BEACON STREET GIRLS

This book belongs to:

VERITAS AMICITIA GAUDIUM
truth friendship fun!

TM

BEACON STREET GIRLS

Be sure to read all of our books:

BSG Special Adventure Books:

Coming Soon:

Isabel's Texas Two-Step

BY
ANNIE BRYANT

ALADDIN MIX

NEW YORK   LONDON   TORONTO   SYDNEY

ALADDIN MIX

An imprint of Simon & Schuster Children's Publishing Division

1230 Avenue of the Americas, New York, NY 10020

Copyright © 2008 by B*tween Productions, Inc.,

Home of the Beacon Street Girls.

Beacon Street Girls, Kgirl, B*tween Productions, B*Street, and the characters Maeve, Avery, Charlotte, Isabel, Katani, Marty, Nick, Anna, Joline, and Happy Lucky Thingy are registered trademarks and/or copyrights of B*tween Productions, Inc.

All rights reserved, including the right of reproduction in whole or in part in any form.

ALADDIN PAPERBACKS, ALADDIN MIX, and related logo

are registered trademarks of Simon & Schuster, Inc.

Designed by Dina Barsky

The text of this book was set in Palatino Linotype.

Manufactured in the United States of America

First Aladdin MIX edition October 2008

4 6 8 10 9 7 5

Library of Congress Control Number 2008931773

ISBN-13: 978-1-4169-6423-0

ISBN-10: 1-4169-6423-1

5543 5993 01/15

Who's Who

BSG

Katani Summers
a.k.a. Kgirl . . . Katani has a strong fashion sense and business savvy. She is stylish, loyal & cool.

Avery Madden
Avery is passionate about all sports and animal rights. She is energetic, optimistic & outspoken.

Charlotte Ramsey
A self-acknowledged "klutz" and an aspiring writer, Charlotte is all too familiar with being the new kid in town. She is intelligent, worldly & curious.

Isabel Martinez
Her ambition is to be an artist. She was the last to join the Beacon Street Girls. She is artistic, sensitive & kind.

Maeve Kaplan-Taylor
Maeve wants to be a movie star. Bubbly and upbeat, she wears her heart on her sleeve. She is entertaining, friendly & fun.

Ms. Razzberry Pink
The stylishly pink proprietor of the "Think Pink" boutique is chic, gracious & charming.

Marty
The adopted best dog friend of the Beacon Street Girls is feisty, cuddly & suave.

Happy Lucky Thingy and alter ego Mad Nasty Thingy
Marty's favorite chew toy, it is known to reveal its alter ego when shaken too roughly. He is most often happy.

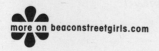

more on beaconstreetgirls.com

Part One
Party Frenzy

CHAPTER

1

Tiara Trouble

I jiggled my foot up and down and stared out the window of Boston's Logan Airport at the jets lined up like toy planes on a game board. To tell the truth I was a little bored, which really wasn't my usual style, particularly since I was about to leave on an adventure.

Then out of the corner of my eye I saw an adorable little boy twirling about like a bird and staring up at the ceiling. As the official BSG artist-in-training, I always reach for my special Isabel Martinez sketchpad whenever I see something different or special to draw. But a burst of girl laughter distracted me for a second.

I glanced over at my sister, Elena Maria, who was deep in important teenage conversation with her chatty best friends, Jill and Lauren. It was pretty obvious that I wasn't going to be invited to join their talk fest. How I wished that Avery, Charlotte, Maeve, and Katani were going to Texas with me. The BSG were my best friends in the world, and right away I wanted to call them and tell them to race to the airport. But I couldn't. This was my sister's adventure. I was just along for the ride. Plus . . . in the morning rush I had forgotten my cell phone at home.

At least I had my art supplies. I felt happy about that. As I leaned down to grab my sketchpad out of the one-of-a-kind artist's bag Katani had sewn for me, it hit me. I mean something actually *hit* me. "Ow!" I squealed. I had just bumped my head on somebody's rising bright orange ankle brace—that somebody being Scott Madden, Avery's older brother, and, I was almost positive, Elena Maria's main crush. Not that she would ever admit that to me in her current state of frenzy. (More about that later.)

"Sorry, Iz, I completely didn't see you reaching down!" Scott said apologetically.

Scott *was* really nice for a high-school guy, even if he had just crashed into my head. I opened my mouth to tell him "No problemo," but before I had the chance, Elena Maria rushed over to his side. "You okay, Scott?" she asked in her sweetest voice. Yup, he was definitely the main crush of the moment.

"Uh, yeah," he said, laughing and sounding a little embarrassed. "I guess a guy with a sprained ankle should be a little more careful."

"I'm okay too—," I started, but was interrupted by Elena Maria's friend Lauren, who called out from across the waiting area, "Check. It. Out! Elena and Scott, you *have* to watch this video Jill has on her iPod! It's sooooo funny!"

Without another look back at me, my sister and a

limping Scott took off to join Jill and Lauren and Scott's friend Andy. I turned to grab some mom attention, but saw that she was sneaking a quick snooze before we boarded. Next to her, my Aunt Lourdes was engrossed in a thick, hardback book.

Again I wished I could chill with the BSG. What an adventure we could have on my aunt and uncle's ranch in Texas. Instead, because it was my sister's superfabulous birthday entitled "My Amazing, Incredible *Quinceañera*," starring Elena Maria Martinez, she got to bring *her* friends.

In our Mexican culture, honoring a girl when she turns fifteen is an important tradition that might even go back all the way to the time of the Aztecs. That celebration is called a *quinceañera*, and it's basically a beautiful ceremony followed by a huge, awesome, rockin' party. I love *quinceañeras* . . . usually. But my sister was taking hers to a whole new level of crazy. All she could talk about was dresses, tiaras, shoes . . . and her amazing party.

The whole *quince* planning thing exploded a couple of months ago when the three of us—Mom, Elena Maria, and me—were sitting in my Aunt Lourdes's living room, looking at some old family photos. I could look at those pictures over and over again and never get sick of them. I loved seeing us all together as a family. Back in the fall we had left our home in Detroit, where my dad still lived, and moved in with Aunt Lourdes in Brookline so Mom could get treated for her multiple sclerosis by doctors in Boston. My aunt was a nurse, and she was tapped into lots of incredible medical care.

Mom's MS was hard to understand and kind of frustrating for me. Sometimes she'd feel okay, and then the next week she might feel weak and dizzy, and there wasn't really a lot we could do about it. But that night had been a good night. Mom was sitting up on the couch and smiling as she held the photo album and flipped through pages of photos of her "darling" daughters.

"Look at this one, Isabel! You were only two years old. And there you are, Elena, just four. My two beautiful girls," Mom said. I scooted closer to the album and giggled at the two of us in our Halloween costumes while Elena Maria filed her nails.

I was surprised that Elena Maria was even hanging out with me and Mom that night. It was a Tuesday, and lately she'd been spending every Tuesday and Thursday evening at Scott Madden's house, "studying Physics," she said.

"Elena," I had teased a few nights earlier, "with the amount of study time you're putting in, your report card should be amazing. Just think," I added, "Mom and Dad will have your report card photocopied and send it to all our relatives in Mexico. The Mexican government will issue a special proclamation declaring it a holiday: 'Elena Martinez, Student of the Century Day'!"

My sister chased me around our bedroom with a spray can filled with purple hair mousse. I was about to get seriously slimed, when I stubbed my toe and started to bleed really, really badly. Elena Maria, who is a total softie inside, grabbed a towel and started treating me like a patient.

"Lean back, Isabel, I'm going to put disinfectant on

your poor toe and bandage you up." Even though the disinfectant hurt like crazy I couldn't help laughing because Elena Maria was acting like Aunt Lourdes. She even took my pulse!

After Nurse Elena fixed me up, we laughed ourselves crazy about Elena Maria Day in Mexico. One of the best things about having my sister is the laugh-a-thons we share over the silly things we do.

After almost a half hour of flipping through the photo album, Elena finally put down her nail file. *Thank goodness,* I thought. The sound of her file scritch-scratching back and forth on her nail had been making me squirm. "Um, so looking at these pictures is fun, but there's something else I think we should talk about," she announced.

Leaning over a huge tote bag, she pulled out an overstuffed white notebook with MY QUINCEAÑERA written in flowery pink letters on the front. Wow! Was I impressed. My sister was really organized for her party.

"You think I looked beautiful as a little girl, Mami? Just imagine me at my *quince!*" She opened the notebook dramatically to reveal pages and pages of pictures torn out of magazines and carefully pasted into the notebook. She had even written little notes on the side of each page about where to buy everything. *So that's what she's been working on,* I thought. For the past few nights she had closed the door to our bedroom after dinner so she could "concentrate."

I smiled politely as she flipped through glossy pages of her ideas for the *quince.* They included: a huge cake, a horse-drawn carriage for her and her court of honor, and an elaborate hairstyle with gobs of curls piled up on top of her head. "That will look sooooo good with the tiara. Have you started thinking about what kind of tiara you want to get me, Mami? Because if you haven't, I have a whole list of choices right here." She flipped to a page where she had pasted a ton of magazine cutouts of the spar most gigantic crowns I had ever seen. I mean, we're t. ing some serious bling.

Before Mom or I could say anything Elena turned to a page covered with pictures of beautiful porcelain dolls. "Don't you just love them, Isabel?" she gushed. "As my little sister, you know I will be giving you my last doll, and believe me, I want to give you the absolute best one I possibly can—but that's up to Mom and Dad, of course," she added, giving Mom a meaningful look.

I looked up at my sister with shining eyes when I heard "the last doll." She knew the last doll was one of my favorite *quinceañera* traditions. In our family, the *quinceañera* sometimes gives her favorite doll or a pretty new doll to a younger sister—like me. It was a sign of approaching maturity.

I was so touched that my sister remembered me in her plans that I restrained myself from giggling at her other way-out plans. I really wanted a last doll. It would be a special symbol of my Mexican heritage and my bond with my sister (even though she can drive me crazy sometimes!), and I would keep it forever.

But then came the shoes. My sister was practically

drooling as she flipped through at least five pages of pictures of every kind of high heel imaginable: strappy, stiletto, kitten heel, hot pink . . . everything. It was another tradition for the *quinceañera*'s father to give her a pair of high-heeled shoes at the ceremony to symbolize how she was growing up, but I'd never seen anyone receive shoes like the ones Elena Maria had picked out! I glanced over at Mom. She was staring intently at the pages, but the corners of her mouth seemed to be twitching.

As Elena continued to page through her notebook, she gabbed at a hundred miles a minute. It was getting harder for me to keep from laughing out loud. "Look at this one, Isabel. Do you see the beads on the toe? And Mom, how adorable is the pink satin strap with three-and-a-half-inch heels? I will look like a model in those." I wanted to tell my sister that she would look like a wobbly flamenco dancer and break a leg in those high shoes, but I didn't. I could tell how important all of this was to her.

Instead I concentrated on my doll. But then I caught Mom's expression and saw that she was about to lose it too. I sat on my hands and began to count birds. *One flamingo, two crows, three robins* . . . birds were my fave. I thought of all the adorable new bird cartoons I could do about flamingos in top hats and tails, crows in wild pink costumes, and fat little robins in tutus. Anything to keep me from bursting out laughing at her outrageous choices.

But then my sister turned the page and pointed to a picture cut from a high-fashion magazine, and dramatically announced what she planned to wear.

"Violet Woo, *peau de soie*, in powder-blush pink. It's only one thousand dollars at Bloomingdale's."

My jaw fell. Mom's eyes popped wide open. "Violet Woo!" I exclaimed. Everyone in the world knew that Violet Woo was one of the most famous fashion designers ever. Elena was so caught up in her dream of pink *peau de soie* that she didn't even register our reactions.

"*Peau de soie* means 'skin of silk' in French," she explained, smiling radiantly. It was like Elena Maria was in some Cinderella world and didn't even realize that her mom and sister thought she had lost her *quinceañera* mind. "It's smooth. They make the fabric some way so it has a finished feel to it on both sides."

I looked at Mom. She bit her lip. I hiccupped . . . and it was all over. Mom and I began to laugh. Quietly at first, but soon I was laughing so hard, I squeezed one of the pillows on the couch so tightly that a feather popped out. That sent my mom over the edge with laughter.

Poor Elena Maria. She looked confused. "What? What's wrong? Do you think I should go with 'Oriental Ivory' instead? What's so funny?"

Mom and I tried to tone it down, we really did. Neither of us wanted to hurt Elena Maria's feelings, but every time one of us tried to speak, the other one would laugh even harder. We were lost in total giggle-riot mode. Everyone knows that when you are in total giggle-riot mode, you have to let it run its course, or you could have a stroke or something.

"Will somebody tell me what's going on?" Elena Maria demanded, sounding hurt.

"*Mi hijita*," Mom finally managed to spit out. "I think you might want to reconsider, at the very least, your choice of gown. A thousand dollars? And a carriage with a team of horses? How could we possibly find a carriage to fit fifteen people?"

"What are you . . . a movie star?" I squealed. I got hit by poison darts coming from Elena Maria's eyes and a warning eyebrow from my mom. I realized I'd better cool it way down. Nobody likes to get made fun of when she's talking about something that is really important to her.

"Mami, this is very serious, and I've done tons of research. I can probably get the gown at Filene's Basement. All the girls tell me it's the place to go for high fashion at bargain prices."

Mom sighed. "Elena Maria, a thousand-dollar dress . . . it's not possible, sweetheart."

"Mami," she cried. "I have to have the Violet Woo. It's perfect! And if they have it at Filene's it'll be much cheaper—maybe half."

"Even that is a bit much."

"A bit much? Considering everything else I need for the *quince*, this is the most reasonable thing I'm asking for."

"Yes, let's consider those other things. The carriage? The doves you want to release? And the live band?" Mom provided answers by shaking her head: No, no, and no. "We need to be more frugal, dear."

"Mami, nooooo! I have to have a carriage! I have to

make my *gran entrada*!" Elena was beginning to sound panicky. I looked over at Mom but she seemed unfazed by my sister's rant. The calmer my mother remained, the wilder Elena Maria became.

Suddenly, Elena dropped her head in her hands. "Why can't I get what I want, just this once?" I really felt sorry for my disappointed sister, even if she was acting like an event planner to the stars.

After a minute of sighing, her head popped up like a pogo stick as she announced, "Which brings me to another important subject. We have to make decisions. Tonight, Mom. Tonight! Deidre sent me an e-mail telling me my friends back in Detroit are waiting for their invitations. At the very least I have to let everybody know when and where, especially the girls and boys on my honor court."

The *quinceañera's corte de honor*, or honor court, was usually made up of seven *damas*, girls, and seven *chambelanes*, boys who acted as the girls' escorts. Plus, some girls also picked one special guy to be their *chambelan de honor*, their date for the big party. I was pretty sure I knew who Elena Maria had in mind.

Mom continued to stare at Elena, with a look of firmness or pity, I couldn't be sure.

"We really need to book the Chateau Celine soon." Elena was still in major *Lifestyles of the Rich and Famous* mode. Mom didn't blink. "We *are* having it at the Chateau, aren't we? Aren't we? Answer me, Mami!" I knew we couldn't afford a place like Chateau Celine, so I braced myself for my sister's freak-out when she heard Mom's answer.

"Elena Maria, please calm yourself, sweetheart . . . and listen to me carefully. We are not having it at the Chateau Celine. Your *quinceañera* is not going to be held in Detroit."

My sister's eyes popped out. "Then let's book it at the Holiday Inn on Beacon Street. I'll call them tonight." Wow, Elena even had plan B ready. I was impressed. She was already an awesome cook, now I could see her future catering business being a huge success. I was pretty excited because if the party was held in Brookline all my friends could come.

But Mom was already shaking her head. "Your *quinceañera* will not be in Brookline, either, dear."

You could have dropped a ten-pound water balloon on Elena Maria's head and she wouldn't have noticed. Or on me, too, for that matter. What was Mom talking about?

Then she surprised both Elena and me with her next announcement. "Your father's sister, your Aunt Inez, and her husband, Uncle Hector, have offered the use of their ranch in Texas for your party. It's all been arranged."

Elena jumped up from the couch. "What? In TEXAS? That's impossible! No way!"

"Please sit down, Elena Maria. Just listen a moment to what your father and I have planned for you. I think you will—"

"I don't want to have my most important birthday at a *ranch* in Texas! That's crazy!" she cried as she wiped a river of tears from her cheeks. "And who's going to be there? My cousins? What about my friends? Who will be my *chambelan de honor*?" she asked. "This has to be a joke! Tell me you're joking. Uncle Hector and Aunt Inez let their chickens run all over the place and everything!"

My reaction was the complete opposite. Texas! Whoa! Chickens. I could barely remember my uncle and aunt's ranch, only that it was in the middle of nowhere, that the house was big and dark, and that there were cows . . . and a rooster. But, wow, what an adventure! "Yee-haw," I yapped. Oops! I clapped my hands over my mouth.

Elena shot me a look. She was not happy with my enthusiasm.

"I think you'll find the ranch has changed a lot since you were last there," Mom explained calmly. "Hector has made a lot of improvements, and I have heard Aunt Inez has decorated the place to the nines. I promise you won't be disappointed with your party."

Elena Maria popped up from the couch and tossed her *quince* book on the floor. In an angry voice she protested, "I am *not* going to Texas for my *quinceañera*. I just won't have one and that's that. If it can't be the way *I* want it, then there won't be one." And then she actually stomped her foot like a two-year-old. I couldn't believe my sister's behavior. Elena Maria had crossed the line, and she knew it, too.

"Elena Maria!" Mom cried forcefully. Whoa. I knew that tone. I looked from Mom's face to Elena Maria's and back again.

After a few seconds of silence, my sister sat back down,

folded her arms across her chest and took a big gulp of air. Mom explained their decision about the party in a patient voice. "Your father and I can't afford to give you the party you want," she said. "But Uncle Hector and Aunt Inez have generously offered to be your *padrino* and *madrina* for the *quinceañera*—to sponsor everything for you. As relatives who care about you very much, they are offering the use of their ranch, catering, the entertainment, and round-trip airfare to San Antonio. You can ask four friends from Brookline to come along.

"Hector and Inez made this offer a couple of weeks ago, and after looking at our budget, your father and I decided that it's really the best option. Your father wanted to surprise you with this together, but it seems that now is the time. We had hoped you would love the idea, but if not, then I am truly sorry."

My mother's words echoed in the air, not so much for what she said, but how she said it. My mom might have MS, but she still has a lot of *fuerza*—force. She sounded strong and very sure of herself.

Elena Maria sighed and looked at the ground. "I guess it'll be okay," she mumbled. But her voice sounded sad. Her party was not what she had dreamed of. I reached over and squeezed her hand. She might be *Quince*-zilla right now, but her eyes were brimming with tears.

"That is a very wise and mature decision, *mi hijita*," Mom said. "Now I am a bit tired." Using her cane, she got up and headed for her bedroom, leaving Elena Maria and me alone on the couch.

I had no idea what to say. "Ummm . . . it'll be so great to see our *primos*," I told her, trying to sound extra-cheerful.

"Oh, Isabel." She sighed. "They don't know anything about anything. Only horses and cows. They're a bunch of *cowboys*." She started sniffling again. "This is awful. I wish I wasn't turning fifteen. Not now."

She sounded so upset. I asked her, "Do you want me to make some special Mexican hot chocolate with cinnamon and whipped cream, and just a little teaspoon of coffee?" It was the only thing I could think of to cheer her up.

"No thanks. I'm not hungry right now. But at least," she said, giving me a little half smile, "I can still ask Scott Madden to be my *chambelan de honor*, so I won't have to dance with my cousins."

Uh-oh. My face gave me away.

"What? Is that a bad idea? Oh, no. He has a girlfriend. Does he, Izzy? Does he have a girlfriend, Izzy?"

"Um, I hate to break it to you, but the dancing part . . . well, Avery told me this morning that Scott had an accident. He fell from the kitchen counter reaching for some spice or something. He might have sprained his ankle . . . really badly."

Elena Maria was silent for a moment, then raised her face and hands to the sky. "*¡Ay, ay, ay!*" she wailed.

CHAPTER

2

The Tango Aeropuerto

I wished my dad could have been here at the airport with us. He could always make me laugh. But Dad wouldn't be flying to Texas until a couple of days before the *quince*, because he had so much work to do.

Suddenly I heard a voice behind me scolding, "Elena Maria! Girls! Will you *please* get your things together?"

I had to laugh. My aunt was attempting to round up all her unruly travelers—but it was like trying to herd baby geese. On the other hand, she was definitely having a good time telling everyone what to do. Aunt Lourdes's favorite thing in life was being the boss . . . of everyone. She was running around in total tour-director mode, doing her best to keep all of Elena's friends in order.

"Boys, please put your video games away now. Andrew, help Scott with his things. We will be boarding this plane any . . . urghh!"

Whoops! My aunt stumbled. Scott the hero, despite his cast, managed to jump up and grab Aunt Lourdes's arm so she wouldn't fall. I had to hand it to that boy. He would be a good *chambelan* for my sister.

"Oh, thank you, Scott," my red-faced aunt said.

"I'm okay, ma'am," he said through gritted teeth. Avery told me that Scott suffered a bad sprain. Jumping up like that must have really hurt his ankle.

I waved to my sister and pointed to Scott. My BFF Avery and I were the ones that got Elena Maria together with Scott in the first place. But my sister ignored me. Hmmm. I sighed. This was going to be one long trip.

Since Scott had managed to save Aunt Lourdes from total embarrassment, she couldn't stop gushing about him. "Scott, you are a true gentleman. Elena, you are so fortunate to have such a wonderful young man for a friend." Elena Maria and Scott turned bright red in front of their friends, who were elbowing each other. Mom, who had been sitting quietly, gave me a wink. I covered my mouth with my hand so Elena wouldn't see me laugh.

"I need to freshen up a bit, and I would like all of you packed up and ready to go when I get back," Aunt Lourdes directed.

"Give me a hand, Andy," Scott said as he went to stand up and stretch.

"How about a foot instead?" Andy asked.

"Thanks, Jim Carrey," Scott quipped.

Completely forgetting Aunt Lourdes's directions, Elena Maria and her two friends went back to looking at our family photo album that Elena insisted we bring. Her friends were going gaga over the pictures.

Whenever Elena Maria got together with a bunch of her friends, it was like the smallest thing made them either totally embarrassed or totally hysterical. They acted like someone dropping a cupcake was the funniest thing known to man. It wasn't that way with me and my friends, the BSG. We laughed when things were really funny, like when Maeve's guinea pig popped out of the salad bowl at Avery's mom's fancy dinner! Now *that* was funny.

"Your cousins are awfully good-looking, Elena," I heard Jill say.

"And these are photos just of the ones who live in San Antonio. Wait till you meet the others who are coming from Mexico. You're gonna think they're completely dreamy," Elena Maria said.

"I'm already in loooove," Lauren said. "If your Mexican cousins are real cowboys like these Texas boys, my heart's going to be beating double time."

Cowboys? Why did Elena Maria keep saying that about our cousins? I certainly didn't remember any of them being cowboys. To be honest, I barely remembered them at all. It seemed like centuries since my last visit.

"Flight two forty-three to San Antonio International Airport will begin boarding in a few minutes." All of a sudden the waiting area was a swirl of activity. Passengers got up and began gathering up their stuff like they were in a mad hatter's tea party. Except for Scott, who seemed as cool as a cucumber. It must be all that traveling that he and Avery do back and forth to visit their dad in Colorado.

"Oh," cried Jill. I turned around to see her frantically

digging through her lavender carry-on bag with BON VOY-AGE printed on the side. "I can't find my wallet. It has all my money in it." She actually started crying. I looked around, not sure what to do.

"Jill, why don't you check all your pockets?" Scott suggested in a real casual tone.

"Yeah," I added. "I always find stuff in my pockets."

"I never put my wallet in my pockets . . . never. Somebody stole my wallet!" she shrieked.

"We're going to miss the plane," Elena Maria cried and began pacing. This situation was getting bad, fast. Thank goodness Aunt Lourdes had gone to the ladies room, or she would have lined everyone up against the wall like an army drill sergeant!

"Really, Jill, check your pockets. My mother forgets and stashes her wallet in her pockets all the time, especially when she is juggling bags and passports at the airport." The ever-patient Scott tried again to calm Jill down. I would have to tell Avery that her brother was one cool dude.

Meanwhile my mother rolled over to Jill in her wheelchair, and in a calm voice began chilling the whole scene out. I loved that about my mom. You could be having a horrible day and my mother could say one little thing, and the next thing you knew everything was okay again.

"Elena Maria, help Jill look in all her pockets," Mom encouraged.

Of course, Jill's wallet was in her jacket pocket, just like Scott suggested.

Aunt Lourdes returned just as the gate attendant announced that it was time to board. By this time, we were all together and ready to go. I threw my sketchbook into my bag and followed everybody to the boarding line. Mom and Aunt Lourdes got to board first, because of my mom being in a wheelchair. I knew everybody was looking at Mom. People always look at people in wheelchairs. Everyone wonders what happened to her.

"Why can't that lady walk?" a little boy asked his mom in a loud voice. Yep, there it was. Even the little kids want to know about people in wheelchairs. I was used to it, because my mom sometimes uses a wheelchair when we go out. I waved to Mom as she went through the line to show everyone that having a mom in a wheelchair was no big deal. She gave me a weak wave back. I was a little worried. She must be tired from all the activity, I thought. I just hoped not too tired. I really wanted my mom to be able to enjoy all the festivities at the ranch.

I tried to stand near them but Aunt Lourdes directed me to fall in line between the three girls and Andrew and Scott. My sister was chatting so fast with Jill and Lauren that I couldn't even tell what they were saying. "Aren't you excited, Elena?" I grabbed her arm.

She said, "Yeah, I am," and turned back to her friends.

Was she ignoring me? We were usually so close. I couldn't believe she didn't want to talk to me. But her friends were huddled in a pack as the line moved on. Elena had her audience enrapt, telling them what to expect once we got to the ranch. I hoped my sister wouldn't ignore me when we got to Texas. I mean, who would I hang around with if not my sister? I didn't know anyone in Texas.

"My cousins took me range riding once. Scott, Andy, maybe Uncle Hector will take us all out to the back pasture and we can practice roping cattle. It's fun! You'll love it," she promised.

"Yee-haw!" Andy shouted in a horrendously bad cowboy accent. "Well now, I reckon that I ain't never been on a horse, and I don't know if my pal, General Scott One-Foot here, can make the trip." Jill smacked him on the arm, and of course they all started laughing hysterically . . . again.

"Move it along, you kids," a man shouted.

It was a good thing that Mom and Aunt Lourdes were already seated. They, especially Aunt Lourdes, would have been annoyed at my sister's friends' antics.

Elena shushed her friends so the man would leave us alone. At least she had *some* sense left. Now was the perfect opportunity to ask if I could use her cell phone. "I want to call Charlotte and tell her that I'm almost on the plane," I explained. "She likes to hear from people at airports. She says that it makes her feel like she's going somewhere, too."

"Where is your phone?"

"I forgot it at home."

"Well, mine is barely charged, so I don't want to use it until we get to Texas."

She and her friends exchanged more giggles about cute cowboys. But my sister must have felt bad because she turned around and added, "You can call the BSG when you get to the ranch."

Urggghhh! How could I explain to Elena Maria with her friends standing there that airports were special to Charlotte. She'd been in so many of them. I promised myself that I would e-mail Charlotte the minute I arrived. When we got on the plane, Elena and her *quince* posse walked straight to the back.

"Come, Isabel." Aunt Lourdes grabbed my arm as I walked by. "Stop here and say hi to your mother. She is snug as a rug in a bug." Aunt Lourdes smiled and I laughed. That was a little joke in our family. Our grand-mother got English phrases like that mixed up all the time, but she had a great sense of humor and could always laugh at herself. I couldn't wait to see her at the *quince*!

I plopped down in the empty seat beside both of them. "Ah, Isabel." Mom grabbed my hand. She had her knitting out and looked happy and relaxed.

"Are you excited, Mami?" I asked.

"Oh, yes. Pretty soon we will be in Texas, my little girl." She reached over and gave my cheek a little pinch. "And eating chiles rellenos that will make your tongue tingle." I was so relieved that she seemed well and bright, I leaned over and laid my head on her shoulder.

All of a sudden I sensed a large person towering over me. "You're in my seat," a man said.

My aunt immediately intervened. "Excuse us. Isabel, take my seat. We have another one a few rows back—I will take that one."

I gave her a grateful smile. Aunt Lourdes to the rescue! But I wanted Aunt Lourdes to sit with Mom and me too. The three of us could play cards together and make our own little group, away from Elena Maria and her *quince*-obsessed posse.

I don't know where I got the nerve, but I stared up at the big man and asked, "Can we exchange seats so I can sit with my mother and my aunt?"

Aunt Lourdes, I could see, was shocked at my boldness, but her eyes were hopeful.

"I need the bulkhead row. I must have the extra room for my legs," he answered in a gruff bear voice. "I'm very tall."

Couldn't he see we needed to sit together? Aunt Lourdes spoke up. "I'll go, Isabel. I'll come back to say hello when we are in the air."

When I saw my mom's disappointed look, I made my decision. "No, that's okay. You sit with Mom. I want to draw in my sketchpad for a while, anyway."

With that I pulled my jacket tight around me and got up. For some reason I wanted my mother and my aunt to see how grown up I was. Plus, I knew the two sisters would enjoy hanging out and talking about the party, and I could totally sit by myself on the plane. I mean, for a twelve-year-old it should be no problem, right?

The man very quickly moved in, whipping a suitcase into the overhead compartment, removing his jacket, and buckling in. I gave my aunt a wave and headed back to my seat alone. I actually felt pretty cool. *Maybe everyone will think I'm a seasoned traveler, like Charlotte.* I smiled at the passengers as I walked down the aisle.

I was eight rows behind my mother and Aunt Lourdes. A college-aged girl was already asleep, and I had to crawl over her. But she was pretty chill about being awakened by my clumsy stumbling. We started chatting. I wanted to yell to Elena Maria, *See, this girl wants to talk to me!*

As we waited for the plane to take off, I could hear my sister and her friends cracking up at the back of the plane and being shushed by someone nearby. I smiled and settled in to do some sketching. Maybe being on my own wasn't so bad after all.

SAN ANTONIO

DEEP, IN THE HEART.

"People laughed and joked as they left the plane ...
Must be the Texas air."

CHAPTER

3

The Stars Shine Bright

The sun had set by the time we landed in San Antonio. People were laughing and joking as they left the plane. Even Aunt Lourdes looked more relaxed. *Must be the Texas air*, I thought. I smiled as I checked that I had put everything back in my bag. I hoped Elena Maria was in a better mood too, and would let me use her cell phone now.

But Elena and her friends were still totally wrapped up in their own world at baggage claim. Jill complained about how hot the airport was. Lauren was disappointed that she didn't see any cowboys around. Scott and Andrew put on their sunglasses and acted like they were a pair of cool dudes from the big city. I noticed that a lot of people — regular people — were walking around in cowboy boots. I really wanted a pair . . . ones with bluebirds on them.

"What's that music piped in overhead?" Scott asked. "It sounds like we should all be holding hands and skipping in a circle or something."

"It's not that at all," Elena Maria answered sharply. "It's Mexican ranch-style music."

"That's a polka! My Polish cousins dance to it all the time," Jill said, laughing.

"No way that's Polish," Scott said. "They're singing in Spanish."

"Well, whatever it is, I like it," Andrew said. He grabbed Jill by the hands and twirled her. "Get used to it, Jill. I hear there's a lot of dancing at kinzy kinzy whatevers."

"Keen-seh-ah-niera!" I piped up.

"And I'm having a band," Elena Maria explained in a haughty voice. "At least there better be one, that plays a lot of hip-hop and soul and funk."

Ugh. One more second of *quinceañera* talk would make me cuckoo. And anyway, I really wanted to let the BSG know that I was in Texas! "Elena, can I please use your cell phone now to text my friends?" I asked.

"Okay."

I was about to take the phone, but all of a sudden we heard a loud whoop. It was my cousin Anthony, the oldest of my Uncle Hector and Aunt Inez's three boys.

"If it ain't the Bostonians! Welcome to Texas, y'all!" His voice boomed throughout the terminal.

"Tony! It's been so long!" Elena ran up to him. The two hugged like they were old friends. This was news to me, but then, she had been to Texas more times than I had.

He was tall. Dark. And from the goo-goo eyes Jill and Lauren were making at him, I could tell they thought he was way handsome. This wasn't the Anthony I remembered. Back then, he was goofy-looking.

When he saw my mother and aunt, he cut through Elena Maria's friends, leaving Jill and Lauren with stars in their eyes and Scott and Andrew looking a little intimidated by this handsome Texas cowboy.

"Tía Lourdes! Tía Esperanza! You ladies look hot!" He gave them big bear hugs. Tony was taller than everybody. His energy seemed to put more color in my mother's cheeks. Then he turned to me.

"Is this *la chiquita*? My little *prima* Isabel? Give your cousin Tony a big *abrazo*, little girl!" And before I knew it, he scooped me up. Whoa! Nobody had actually picked me up in years! These Texas boys were enthusiastic. I grinned from ear to ear.

After all the introductions, Tony said his mom had a big dinner waiting for us at the ranch. Since my stomach was growling, that was welcome news to me. I wondered how we were all going to fit in one vehicle, but when we got outside he pointed to a big, shiny, black Suburban SUV, the kind with three rows of seats and little TVs hanging from the ceiling. All the girls hurried to get a seat. "You're not going to believe the inside," Jill shouted to the boys, who were struggling to get all the luggage into the back of the car or lashed onto the roof.

"My mother is so excited about your *quinceañera*, Elena," Tony explained after we got on the road. "She and Dad are thrilled you're letting them do this for you. You know, my mother, she's always wanted a girl of her own.

Guess me and Fonzie and Rico weren't cute enough." He laughed.

Elena Maria was silent. There was something about his words "letting them do this for you" that made her clam up. The awkward silence was broken by Lauren.

"Fonzie? Rico? Who're they?"

"Didn't Elena Maria tell you? Those are nicknames for my younger brothers, Alfonso and Ricardo. Don't tell them I told you, though."

Jill and Lauren exchanged sly looks. "We won't." They giggled in unison. I got the feeling that my cousins might be in for some girl trouble.

Sandwiched between Scott and Andrew in the far back row, I couldn't really see out the windows, but the scenery must have been interesting because both boys had their faces pressed against the glass. Meanwhile, Tony continued to act like our tour guide.

"We're heading due west of San Antonio. I think you Boston folks will find *Rancho Los Mitotes* very comfortable, with everything you need. Mama's set it up so that the guys'll stay with us in the north wing, and the girls and the two *tías* in the south."

Jill and Lauren grinned and looked at each other. I knew exactly what they were thinking. "Wings" equaled mansion! Mansion equaled swimming pools and princess-style bedrooms. I had to admit, I was excited too.

"Tell my friends more about your place, Tony," Elena Maria said, practically glowing.

"Oh, Elly-belle. That can wait. Believe me, you're all

going to hear a lot more about our place than you'll ever want to know."

"Come on! Tell them. They're going to go absolutely nuts." She turned to her friends. "You are going to *love* this place."

Tony laughed, cleared his throat, and told a story he'd obviously told many times.

"We moved there when Rico was still tiny, about five years old. You know, big ears, missing teeth. He was a yuuugly little thing."

Boys, I thought.

My mom asked Tony to go on with his story. Tony beeped his horn at a big Cadillac emblazoned with a long-horn steer hood ornament and then continued. "We used to have a tiny ranch, just about a hundred acres further south from here, until we discovered a small pocket of natural gas on the property. My dad immediately sold it when we found this place. It's called *Rancho Los Mitotes. Mitotes* is a Spanish word for dances. Wait, maybe it's an Indian word. Anyway, it was used to describe the parties that the local people had a long time ago. They'd have feasts and drink and dance and do all sorts of festive things. Supposedly, our land was such a place where the Coahuiltecan people would gather."

"Kwo-weel-whaaat?" Andy piped up.

"It's pronounced 'kwo-weel-tek-ahn.' They were peaceful, and they sometimes lived side by side with the Spanish at the missions. We've never found artifacts or anything that proves they were there, but we know this ranch was established in the late 1800s. It already had its name by the time we came along, so there might be something to the rumor that it was a special place for the Coahuiltecans.

"Our ranch is unique in that, at the north end, the terrain is Hill Country, with a bunch of live oaks and small hills, and to the south, it's mostly flat land—scrub, cactus, mesquite, stuff like that."

Scott leaned over and high-fived Andrew. I guessed they both thought they would be riding the range like old-time cowboys or something. The thought of all these city slickers dressed in chaps and hats appealed to my ridiculous side. I saw a cartoon in the making.

"Antonio," my mother said in Spanish, "tell them about the cattle operation."

"Sure, Tía. We've had a small cattle ranching business for about six years now. We specialize in Brahmans, and when you see them, you might find them a little strange-looking. But the beef is tasty and our cattle are known as the best around. We also have some Charolais, Red Angus, Herefords, and oh, I almost forgot—Elly-belle, you're going to like this—we've got a few longhorn steers now. They're really cool."

"Oh, no. I don't like that at all!" Elena Maria protested. "The last time I was there, I almost got chased down by a big, mean cow! I don't like cows with horns."

"Well, then you're really going to like our newest additions, the mini Hereford."

"Can you ride them?" Lauren asked.

I smacked my forehead. "Even I know you can't ride

a cow!" Elena Maria put her finger up to her mouth. That was her signal to tell me not to embarrass her friends. I was beginning to think that I might not get anything right with my sister this week.

Tony thought about this. "Well, I guess you can, but they won't go very far. They just sorta stand around and . . . chew cud." Tony looked at my mother. "Tía Esperanza, my father is going to ask you if you'd like to serve barbecue at the fiesta. He's famous for his barbecue."

Lauren and Jill let out a collective gasp. "We love barbecue!"

"Yum," Elena Maria exclaimed. "Sounds great, Tony!"

"Tony," I yelled from the backseat. "Is that natural swimming hole, the cavern or whatever it's called, still there?"

"The *tinaja*? Yes, it is, but if you want to go swimming, we've now got something better—a great, big, new swimming pool!"

My mother gasped. "*Ay*, Antonio. I'll bet that was your mother's idea."

"You got that right, Tía. Mom has wanted one for so long that Dad had one installed last Mother's Day. She never liked the *tinaja*. But I liked it. In the swimming hole, the water's always cool and most of the time, clean.

"Isabel," he yelled to the backseat. "We've had a lot of rain this spring, but the waterfall isn't running yet."

I clearly remembered the *tinaja*. It had this cool limestone outcropping that formed a half dome over the pool.

When I was little it looked to me like the kind of place where fairies and talking animals would have tea parties.

The city was far behind us, and the night sky was filled with stars. Soon everybody grew quiet. The twinkling sky stretched before us.

Andrew broke the silence. "Wow. I can't believe how many stars are out tonight."

"Dude," Tony said proudly, "you're deep in the heart of Texas!"

CHAPTER

4

Mi Casa Es Su Casa

Mom and Aunt Lourdes spoke quietly in Spanish with Tony as we drove toward open country. Tony's command of Spanish made him sound like a native Mexican speaker. I loved hearing the musical sounds.

"I hope everybody's hungry! Fidencia and Enrique, our *cocineros*—that's cooks—have been cooking all day. And here we are," he said, turning off the highway. He brought the Suburban to a full stop and clicked a button. Like "open sesame," I saw a big iron gate, illuminated in the headlights, swing open.

"Look at Tony," Elena Maria whispered. "He's still such a kid."

"He's such a *cute* kid," Lauren cooed.

"Lauren, put your eyeballs back into their sockets," Andrew teased.

We were still laughing when we pulled up to the main house. A small crowd had gathered to welcome us. I saw my Uncle Hector and Aunt Inez, and a guy I guessed was my cousin Alfonso, who was clowning around with a younger boy who had to be his little brother, Ricardo. Standing next to them was a very short and plump couple. The *cocineros*, I thought. Better steer clear of them—they looked as serious as if they were at cooking school, about to take the biggest test of their lives!

Everybody stumbled out of the car with a lot of commotion. I heard a deep gasp. "Just look here," a lively female voice said. It was Aunt Inez. She pushed through the group, grasped both my hands, and bent over to put her face in mine. "*Mira esta muchachita. ¡Que hermosa!* This can't be the little rag doll named Isabel! You were just a tiny thing when I last saw you."

All of a sudden I was lost in her warm hug, trying to breathe through her flowery perfume. I couldn't help myself. I started to cough.

"Just look at that hair, those beautiful eyes. Isabel, you're the spitting image of your father," she said. I had not remembered much about Aunt Inez at all. Now I didn't see how I could have forgotten her! She wore her thick, black hair in a tight bun, with blue eye makeup and lots of shiny silver jewelry. She was pretty but a little overdone, in my opinion. My friend Maeve would have loved her.

She let me go as abruptly as she had cornered me. "Speaking of which, when does Jorge arrive? We have to ensure that he learns the waltz for Elena Maria's *entrada*. Though I doubt he'll have any trouble. What a *bailador*!"

"What does *bailador* mean?" Jill whispered to Elena Maria.

"It means 'dancer,' my dear," Aunt Inez explained. "And I think in the dictionary it will have Jorge's picture next to the definition!"

Everyone laughed and started moving into the house. "Hey, Elena, do you want to . . ." I started, but trailed off. She was chatting to Jill, not even listening to me. Would my sister even remember I was here? I hung back, not sure what to do next.

"Hi, Isabel."

My cousin Ricardo, hands in his pants pockets, was shuffling one foot against the floor, head hanging down. He shyly looked up. We hadn't seen each other in almost eight years. I didn't remember him looking so . . . goofy.

"Ricardo?"

"Yehhhh," he answered. I searched for something familiar about him. When did he sprout such a thick mop on his head? Why such thick eyeglasses? There it was—the ears—peeking through his crop of hair.

"Do you remember me?" he asked.

"Yeah, sure," I said. More silence. I fidgeted with my bag.

"Are you hungry? Let's go eat," he said finally.

"Okay," I answered, instantly relieved. Food was becoming a priority! I didn't like the sandwich on the plane, so I was starving.

The Saddest Princess

The dining room had the longest table I'd ever seen, and it was all set for a delicious dinner. The salsa was already on the table. Yum! I couldn't wait to dip into that. Salsa was one of my favorite snacks—the hotter, the better. At least six more people could have joined us after everybody sat down. Fidencia proudly ladled out scoops of steaming red rice, and at one end of the table, Uncle Hector sliced a huge barbecued brisket. Aunt Inez rattled off a list of completed arrangements.

"The menu is planned, the flowers ordered, and your cousin Miguel, Esperanza—the priest—will lead us in a simple ceremony behind the old barn."

"Behind the barn? Won't it be a little . . . stinky?" Elena Maria asked as she wrinkled her nose.

"Elena!" my mother gasped.

But Tía Inez just chuckled. "No, don't worry, dear. We use the old barn for storing tools and your uncle keeps an office in there. I've been landscaping the area by the southwest corner for years, because you can see beautiful sunsets from there. There is also a gorgeous, huge, and ancient live oak. Take a look at it tomorrow morning. I think you'll agree that it's a perfect site."

She turned back to my mother and Aunt Lourdes and said in an excited voice, "We commissioned a local family to make some benches and a water fountain out of *faux bois*. This particular family's work has become incredibly popular in this area."

My mother's eyebrows rose. Aunt Lourdes looked away.

"It's perfect! Only the best for my dear niece," Aunt Inez continued. She gazed at Elena Maria. "I've been dreaming about your *quinceañera* for years, *mi amorcita.* *¡Ay!* I have no daughters, but I'm fortunate, thanks to God, to have plenty of nieces. Elena, I hope you are the first of many who will have their *quince* here."

My sister glowed under my aunt's enthusiasm. She stood and walked to Aunt Inez, wrapped her arms around her neck and gave her a kiss on the cheek. "You're the best, Tía."

Was that a tear coming from Aunt Inez's eye? What was that sneaky glance between my mom and Aunt Lourdes about? Jill and Lauren looked like they were in the presence of a saint. Aunt Inez and Elena Maria were having a love fest.

When dinner was over, Aunt Inez stood up and announced the sleeping arrangements. She asked her sons to show Scott and Andrew to their rooms, and told the girls and Mom and Aunt Lourdes to follow her. She rattled off some instructions in Spanish to Fidencia, who nodded and walked toward me. I could see that all of Elena Maria's friends were really impressed. And Elena—she was so proud. As she walked away from the table, she tossed her long hair over her shoulder and said to Scott, "Isn't this a beautiful home?"

At first I was annoyed with my sister, thinking she was going to make my parents feel bad because they couldn't provide such a beautiful space for their daughter's *quince.* But then I remembered something my father said after I won an art competition in third grade. The girl who came in second was crying, and I wanted to give her my award to make her feel better. My dad said, "Everyone needs their time in the sun. Isabel, this is yours. Please enjoy it. Your little friend will have her time." I figured that the whole *quinceañera* was Elena Maria's time in the sun. I would just have to be patient with her party drama.

"*Venga, niña,*" Fidencia said, grabbing my elbow.

Once again, I was confused. "But . . . ," I said, in English, trying to catch Mom's eye. But Aunt Lourdes was already whisking her away.

"*Sí, sí,*" Fidencia said sweetly. I didn't leave my chair.

Aunt Inez said, "Isabel, we have a bed for you in the old nursery, next to our housekeeper, Mercedes's, room. It is so charming. I just know you will just love it. I will be there soon to get you settled."

Enrique stood nearby, ready to wheel my suitcase. It felt weird to be escorted to a room that was so far away from everybody else. The two cooks walked on either side of me. I was beginning to feel like a lonely princess being led to a solitary tower. Enrique wouldn't even let me roll my own luggage. I liked carrying my own stuff. It always made me feel like I could manage.

I followed Fidencia up some stairs to the second floor, then came to the end of a long hall that turned into another short flight of stairs. I heard a radio blasting more of the accordion music from a nearby room as we turned the corner.

"*¿Esa música, que es?*" I managed to ask.

"Eh?" Fidencia answered. I guessed my accent sounded funny to her.

"The music. *La música. ¿Que es—?*"

"Ah! *La música*," she said. She ducked into the room and spoke in Spanish to whomever was inside. The radio shut off instantly. I peeked inside and saw an attractive woman standing over an ironing board. She was probably Mercedes, the housekeeper my aunt had referred to earlier. She looked nice, and I gave her a little wave.

Fidencia hummed until we reached a door. Enrique reached in his pocket and pulled out a key to unlock it. Then they said good night and left.

The room was small, but it was very pretty and "charming," as Aunt Inez said, in a quiet, spare kind of way. It reminded me a bit of the Tower back at Charlotte's house in Brookline because it was a strange shape. Three of the white walls had tall, narrow windows, hidden by closed wooden shutters. A kid-size bed covered with a beautiful quilt was pushed against one wall. Next to the bed was a small, painted wooden table. On top of the table was a pink candle in a glass container and a pretty white lamp in the shape of a cookie jar.

I took out a family photo I'd tucked into my sketchpad and laid it against the lamp. I felt a little settled now, but still I wondered where in the house my mom was staying.

Suddenly Aunt Inez bustled in. "Isabel, you can put your clothes in the chest of drawers. There is a bathroom at the other end of the hall. I think you'll be quite comfortable here, dear." She gave me a kiss on the cheek.

As she turned to walk out the door, I asked, "Tía? Where are Mom and Aunt Lourdes?"

She looked at me for a second before answering. "They're downstairs on the opposite side of the house. Your mother should not be climbing stairs, you know, and Lourdes needs to be near her, just in case. Mercedes is right next door if you need anything." *Need anything?* Did Aunt Inez remember that my Spanish needed work? How was I supposed to talk to Mercedes?

I nodded, even though what she said made no sense to me. "Tía, is there a computer I might use?"

"Computer! *¡Muchacha!* It's much too late for that. We have a busy day tomorrow. We must shop for some items for the honor court. It's bedtime for you, my dear."

Bedtime? It couldn't be later than nine o'clock! I was surprised by how bossy my aunt was. Even more than Aunt Lourdes. I hoped bossy wasn't some gene that ran in the family.

She gave me another swift kiss good night and mumbled some blessings in Spanish in my ear. "Get some sleep."

"I want to say good night to Mom."

"Your mother is already asleep. She's had such a long day. Now the best thing you can do for her is go to bed yourself." She left, closing the door behind her.

Oooookay. I almost felt like crying. There was no TV and I had nothing to read; I had only my sketchpad. But I didn't feel particularly creative. I kicked off my shoes and put on my slippers.

With nothing else to do, I started to unpack and soon heard voices coming from the room next door. I stuck my head out the door. It was Ricardo, talking in Spanish to Mercedes.

"Isabel, they put you way over here?" he said when he saw me. "That's so bogus. There's a party going on in the billiards room."

"Your mom told me to go to sleep." I wasn't sure I wanted to hang out with Ricardo. He seemed to think he was all that, and I didn't want to get in trouble with my Aunt Inez.

"Get outta here. It's way too early, Izzy. Come on, I'll show you around," he said, like he was king of the castle or something.

I hesitated.

"Don't worry, my mom really won't care. She likes a party. The grown-ups have all gone to their side of the house, anyway. Come on!" Sides of the house? A billiards room? This place really was a castle!

I followed him through hallways filled with beautiful Mexican-style rugs. Soon we were in front of a huge door that Ricardo said was the entrance to the *sala*. He opened the door and flipped on switches to various lights. "You like art, right, Isabel? Check this out."

I was almost speechless. The room was right out of a decorating magazine. If my friends Maeve and Katani, the two BSG who most loved style and fashion, were here, they would have been swooning.

The room was bathed in a soft light and there were several sitting areas—long leather sofas and deep, plushy velvet chairs in a dark red at one end, a beautifully carved gaming table and Spanish-style leather bucket chairs at the other. But what I really noticed was the art. My fingers start to tingle. Inspiration was everywhere. There was a stunning bronze statue of a cowboy on horseback, a collection of old silver spurs in a glass cabinet, ornate Victorian lamps with smoky stained-glass shades. I felt like I was in a museum.

When I looked up at the dark wood walls my heart skipped a beat. The massive painting before me looked familiar: a very happy man in a bright blue suit, holding a watermelon slice on his lap. The background was an eye-popping hot pink.

"It's an early Rufino Tamayo," Ricardo rattled off, like he was repeating something he'd heard his mom say a million times. "And that's an original Diego Rivera over there."

I spun around. Diego Rivera, the husband of my absolute favorite artist, Frida Kahlo! I walked over to get a closer look. The picture was of a little girl in a polka-dot skirt receiving a bundle of golden flowers from a woman seated on the floor, wearing Indian clothing. The girl looked shy, the woman sad. I held my breath. I had never been that close to the work of such a famous artist before. I knew better than to reach out and touch it.

"It's called 'Mother's Helper,'" Ricardo said. "My father gave it to my mother this past Christmas."

"Oh my gosh!" I was thunderstruck. "I can't believe you actually have a Diego Rivera painting in your house! All this is Mexican art, right?" I waved my hand about.

Ricardo nodded as he jumped up and down on the leather sofa like it was a trampoline. Boys were so weird sometimes. It never would have occurred to me to jump on such a nice couch. At least he'd taken off his shoes. When he jumped back onto the floor, his hair stuck out all over the place.

"I guess so. Most of it is, anyway. Look at these sculptures. They're made by a famous lady from Mexico, Josefina Aguilar. Some of them are really funny." He ran to a corner of the room and pushed a button. A light shone on a table that had about a dozen clay figures. They were simple statues, crudely made, but colorful and eye-catching. One was of a woman holding a bunch of calla lilies. Another was obviously Frida Kahlo. She had a parrot on one shoulder, a monkey on the other, and a cigarette in one of her hands.

"I know who this is," I said.

"Yeah, who doesn't?" Ricardo answered smugly. Sometimes Ricardo was nice, but sometimes . . .

Then a big glass statue of a bird caught my eye. When I walked closer, I realized it was an image of the Mexican national emblem. An eagle with a giant wingspan stood on a branch of prickly pear cactus, grasping a snake with one of its talons and its beak. The eagle's eye was deeply polished. It looked almost like a black diamond. For a second, I wondered if the eagle could fly.

I'd seen this image a thousand times, on everything from Mexican coins to the Mexican flag. But never like this, with such expression. The eagle's wings were so detailed I could make out the lines on individual feathers. The snake had scales so thick it looked like it had a plate of armor on, even if it was only made of glass.

"I love this," I said, and reached out my hand.

"But you better not touch it." Ricardo stopped me. "That one's new. It's pretty cool, I guess," he went on casually. "My mom just got it from some famous artist." He acted as if that was no big deal to have a sculpture from a famous artist. I ignored him. I just couldn't take my eyes off the statue. "Do you know the story behind the emblem?" he asked me.

"I can't remember the whole thing," I said and turned away. I suddenly felt tired, and Ricardo was starting to get on my nerves a little. Like now. He wanted to give me a history lesson.

"Well, it represents the founding of Mexico. The ancient Aztecs were a nomadic tribe. It was foretold they could not settle until they came across an eagle on top of a cactus, feasting on a snake. Well, they found it all right, on an island in the middle of Lake Texcoco. So they started building but soon crowded out the island. They built land extensions, called *chinampas*, over the water to make room for more people and to grow food, by moving dirt and stuff to fill in the lake. Pretty soon the place was huge."

"Ricardo, did you learn all this at school?" I was kind of impressed at how much he knew.

He shook his head. "I read about it in this book I have. Mexico City was built on a lake. That's why a lot of its old buildings are sinking." I remembered that my grandfather told me that. "Crazy, huh? That one of the world's largest cities was built on mud? But in the olden days, it was called Tenochtitlán," he explained.

"Boston was sort of built the same way," I told him. "Except in the 1800s, they used wooden pilings, like big telephone poles, to extend the land into the bay. Parts of the city, like the Back Bay, were built right where the water used to be." I paused, and asked him, "How do you know so much about Mexican history?"

"Isabel, look where you live. You're way up in the north. Down here, you practically can't forget for a second that this was once Mexico."

I nodded again, realizing that Ricardo was one smart kid. I took one last look around the room before he started to turn out the lights. My eyes lingered on the huge paintings. "Wow. Those paintings are pretty cool, but that statue—I love birds. This is my favorite piece in the whole room," I said.

"Yeah, of all the stuff we've got here—and believe me, my mom likes to buy a lot of art—it's my favorite too. She says she'll keep buying stuff until she has to do the dusting. But for now, Mercedes does all that."

I wanted to e-mail the BSG and tell them I was sleeping under the same roof that housed a Diego Rivera painting, with cooks and a housekeeper and a magical glass eagle to guard the house. Ricardo had the biggest smile on his face. He knew I was impressed, and he was obviously eating it up. I guessed this was his time to shine a little.

Finally I said, "Your family must be *really rich*."

He shook his head, like he was embarrassed. "If you say so."

"Um, is there a computer I can use, for just a few minutes?" I asked.

"Why?" he asked. What was with everybody here? It was like no one wanted me to make contact with the outside world.

"I just want to touch base with my friends, the BSG," I explained in a kind of whiny way. I was starting to feel pretty tired, and I really wanted to talk to my best friends before I went to bed. "I have to give them my first impressions of Texas and life on the ranch. It's this cool thing we do sometimes. Like if we are experiencing something new we have to tell each other what we think, and then a week later see if we still feel the same way. It's really kind of funny." Ricardo looked unimpressed, but I kept going anyway.

"For example," I continued. "The first time my friend Avery tasted my sister's mole sauce, she about gagged. She said it tasted like chocolate chalk. A week later she said it tasted worse, like chocolate dirt. My friend Charlotte, who has been to a lot of different places, loved it. She wanted my sister—"

"You sure talk a lot, Isabel," he interrupted.

"Whatever." Boys . . . it's like they can only handle listening to a certain number of words before their brains shut down.

"Come on, Isabel, we better split before we get caught in here." *Get caught!* Had Ricardo broken a house rule or something? I looked around, suddenly afraid that a fiery Tía Inez might come flying through the door on a broom.

"Ricardo, why did you bring me in here when you weren't supposed to?" I spun around to walk out. Unfortunately for the art world, Ricardo, and me, as I lifted my arm up, my sleeve caught on the glass eagle. Before I realized what was happening, the glass sculpture started to tip.

What happened next was like one of those terrible movie scenes where time stands still before the whole scene explodes. As if in slow motion, the eagle fell forward. Both Ricardo and I went in for the save as I yelped, "Ah!"

For one terrible second it was touch-and-go. A vision of the eagle smashed to smithereens on the floor buzzed through my head. But lucky for us, we managed to keep the huge sculpture from hitting the floor. In relief, we both sighed and began to giggle at the same time. And then we stood up. *Huge* mistake! *Huge!* The eagle's wing nicked the table, and the glass tip flew across the room.

"Isabel, look what you did!" Ricardo accused.

"That's not fair!" I practically screamed. "You made me come in here."

A guilty look crept across his face.

"Well, what do we do now?" I was nearly in tears. The thought that I might have ruined my sister's *quince* and put my family in debt forever was beginning to form in my spinning brain.

"I have an idea." He paused.

"What?" I asked, thinking that my cousin was going to

tell me to hide the sculpture under my bed or something ridiculous like that.

"You're an artist, right?" he asked hopefully.

"Yeah." Even though I didn't consider myself a real artist yet, and I wasn't sure where he was going with his question, I was hoping against hope that his idea was a good one.

"How about we glue the piece back on? You can make it look really clean and everything."

I opened my mouth to protest, but I was too freaked out to think of anything better to do, so I said, "Okay." Then I remembered the poor eagle. "Do you think that we can lift this back onto the table? My arms are killing me."

"You're funny, Isabel," he said with a laugh as we gently rested the beautiful bird on the table. I was beginning to feel really sad. I had just ruined an incredible piece of art. Would my family ever forgive me? More important, would the art world?

Ricardo slunk out of the room to find some glue while I went in search of the glass tip. Fortunately it was resting, intact, under the chair facing the fireplace. I carefully picked it up and polished it off with my sleeve. "Bad sleeve," I scolded. "Look at all the trouble you caused." I sadly carried the broken piece back to the table.

"I am so sorry, beautiful eagle," I whispered to the amazing glass bird, which almost felt alive in my hands. I tried to fit the shimmering tip back on the wing and said softly, "I hope you will forgive me for damaging your beauty." Art meant everything to me, and thinking that

I had broken this wonderful work made me want to cry with shame.

Lucky for Ricardo and me, the break was a clean one, and perhaps the glue would work. I sat down in the leather chair facing the fireplace to wait for his return. A smidgen of hope was starting to creep into my brain.

Suddenly I heard the doorknob turn behind me. I slunk deep in the seat and made myself as small and invisible as I could. Then I crossed my fingers. *Please let it be Ricardo, please, please.*

It wasn't.

"Who left these lights on?" Tía Inez huffed. She paused. I figured she was looking around the room, and I prayed she couldn't see me. I held my breath when I heard her step farther into the room. She was quiet for another moment, then Aunt Inez spoke softly. "Good night, beautiful art. Thank you for gracing our home."

Suddenly it was dark.

I pinched myself just to make sure I was still alive and had heard right. Tía Inez was a true art lover, not one of those people who buy art for decoration. I leaned my head against the back of the chair. *Will my aunt ever forgive me for ruining her sculpture?* I wondered.

The doorknob turned again, but this time I was too exhausted and guilty to move. If it was Tía Inez again, I would just have to throw myself on the floor and beg for mercy.

"Isabel?" Thankfully, it was Ricardo's voice. I turned around to see him walk into room, a bottle of glue in his hands. *Phew.* Together, we managed to do a fair job of gluing the tip back on.

"Isabel, we better not tell anyone about this," he said in a worried tone.

"Ricardo, what if someone notices? What then?" I looked him in the eye.

"They won't. We aren't even going to use this room for the *quinceañera*. By the time somebody notices, the *quince* will be over, and . . ." He stopped midsentence and looked at me with a funny expression on his face. I don't think he totally believed what he was saying.

Both of us tiptoed silently out of the room.

Before he went to his own room, Ricardo grabbed my hand and gave it a squeeze. "We're in this together, Isabel. We have to stay loyal."

"Ricardo, we have to tell someone . . . soon," I said as I let go of his hand. I walked back to my "charming" little bedroom, far away from everyone. I could hear my sister and her friends in the billiards room laughing it up. I was thankful to be alone, because I planned on crying myself to sleep. My sister's happiest time had turned into one of the worst days of my life.

Later, as I fell asleep to the sounds of accordion music coming through the wall from Mercedes's room, I thought about all the ways to confess. My favorite was having Ricardo confess and take all the blame . . . but I knew I wouldn't really let that happen.

CHAPTER

5

Pink Dresses
and Blue Turtles

ock-a-doodle-dooooo!"

For a second my sleepy brain didn't register the sound. "Go back to sleep, Elena," I mumbled, burying my head in a pillow. Then I remembered . . . I was in Texas! And what I was hearing was a real rooster!

It took me about a split second to get to the windows. The light coming through had colored the room golden yellow. I ran from one window to the next, throwing open all the shutters, and saw before me the landscape that was . . . *my uncle's ranch.*

There were low buildings in one direction, and nearby, a fenced-in corral. To the right I saw the corner of a swimming pool, sparkling in the morning sun. I saw cows in the distance. I raised one of the glass windows and inhaled.

"Yeeeee-haaaaw," I started, realizing my cowgirl cheer needed some serious work to sound authentic. But I would definitely have some time to perfect it here. The morning was cool, quiet, and I felt so happy . . . until I remembered the broken eagle. I forced myself to put the image of a cracked eagle wing out of my mind. It was such a beautiful day, I didn't want to miss any of it.

I dressed quickly and headed toward the kitchen, running my fingers along the bumpy stuccoed walls of the long hallway. The texture of the walls appealed to me and I imagined having walls like that in own home someday. I passed an empty dining room and skipped into the kitchen.

Fidencia faced the stove, her slapping hands letting me know I'd soon be feasting on fresh tortillas. Mmm! I couldn't wait. Mercedes sat at the prep table, slicing and mincing a mound of vegetables and herbs. She was sipping a cup of steaming Mexican coffee. The smell of cinnamon made my nose twitch with pleasure. Soft accordion sounds came from a radio nearby.

"*Buenos días,*" I said.

Both ladies fussed over me like mother hens, rushing me with questions. Hungry? Thirsty? Did you sleep well? What does the *preciosa* need? Their fawning was just what I needed, and a pleasant warmth came over me. I didn't know what to answer first. There were so many choices.

Suddenly I heard the rooster crow, and it sounded so close it scared me out of my wits! "Eeeee!" I shrieked as I felt a little peck on my ankle. I couldn't believe it—that naughty rooster was under the kitchen table!

"*¡Pecas! ¡Fuera!*" Fidencia grabbed a broom and shooed

the bird out the door, which was propped open with a rock.

"*¿Le llamas 'Pecas'?*" I asked. What a weird name for a rooster. "Freckles?"

"*Sí, sí,* Freckles. *Muy travieso, ese gallo, el Pecas,*" Mercedes said.

Travieso. Now there's a word I hadn't heard in a while. It meant troublemaker. Would my aunt think I was a troublemaker when she found out about the broken eagle?

As if on cue, Aunt Inez appeared. She was perfectly groomed and wore lots of beautiful turquoise jewelry. "My darling, you're up early," she greeted me. "Did you sleep well? Everybody else is still in bed."

"Good morning! I slept fine. Tía, what lovely jewelry! And did you know that my room changes colors?" I was babbling, but I was afraid. I wanted to tell her about the eagle, but I had promised Ricardo not to say anything just yet.

She looked at me funny and said, "You have the eye of an artist, I see. Light is so important to how color is interpreted." Then she clapped her hands—I was so nervous I almost jumped!—and proclaimed, "We're going to have a full day, *mi 'jita.* Breakfast will be served shortly after eight, so have some lovely strawberries or cereal in the meantime, please. Mercedes will be knocking on everyone's door soon to get us going." And then she flew off like an . . . eagle?

The day's activities were announced at the breakfast

table. All the ladies were going to San Antonio's famous River Walk, a colorful area of shops and restaurants that is one of the most popular tourist sites in Texas. I had read all about the art galleries that lined the streets. I shivered in anticipation.

"Afterwards," Aunt Inez announced, "we will have lunch at the revolving Tower of the Americas restaurant." Then she read such a long shopping list of *quinceañera* items that it made me dizzy.

"I hope I'm up to one of Inez's marathon shopping sprees," Mom teased with a laugh. But I knew she was worried about keeping up.

Uncle Hector came in, pushing a folded compact wheelchair before him. "For you, Esperanza. Just in case," he added with a smile. "This is very light and easy to pull along."

Mom looked genuinely touched. "How thoughtful, Hector. Now I can really shop until I drop!" she said with a laugh. *I know what my job is today*, I thought. I loved pushing Mom in her wheelchair, because it made me feel like I was important—like I was really helping her.

Uncle Hector cleared his throat. "*Muchachos*, honored guests of my precious niece Elena Maria, today I am treating you to a tour of San Antonio's missions. Some ruins of the old missions can be found on this property. We will return here for lunch, and then my sons will be happy to show you around our modest ranch."

Scott and Andrew high-fived each other, relieved to

miss the shopping expedition. I knew nothing about the San Antonio missions, but they sounded way more interesting than shopping for more *quinceañera* stuff. I looked at my mother, whose eyebrows said, *Don't even think of asking*. Given my adventures the night before, I dared not utter one ounce of complaint about anything. No, today . . . I would be mature, as befitting a member of my sister's court.

Shop Till You Drop

During the drive to the River Walk, Aunt Inez rambled on about the origins of San Antonio. But her history lesson, like Ricardo's, was actually pretty interesting. Aunt Inez was beginning to grow on me. She seemed to have so many passions—art, history, shopping. . . .

"As the Spaniards moved northward from Mexico," she told us, "Franciscan friars enlisted local Indians to help them build forts. A string of protective settlements were established along a river. These included *presidios*, or outposts, and missions, which were religious communities. One of them, the Mission San Antonio de Valero, would become the heart of the city. That mission was closed in 1793 and eventually became known as the Alamo, probably named after a regiment of soldiers that was later stationed there.

"The Alamo is the best known of all the missions, but in my opinion, the least impressive," she said. "But it's on the River Walk, next to the mall that we're going to."

"Will we get to see it?" I asked hopefully.

"If we have time, but I doubt it," she said.

I now could see what I'd missed last night on the ride from the airport. As we got closer to the city center, the roads gave way from neighborhood clusters of one-story wood-frame houses to modern office towers.

"Everything is so spread out here," Jill said. "And look at that old movie theater, the Alameda. It looks like it's frozen in time."

"Elena, are your cousins who make up the rest of your honor court going to wear something different from us?" Lauren asked.

"The dresses have been ordered for the *damas*," Aunt Inez answered before Elena Maria could even open her mouth. "Lauren, Jill, you two will be fitted today. Elena Maria, I have some choices already in mind for you. But, of course, you get to make the final selection." My aunt and my sister beamed at each other.

I glanced over at my mom, who was staring out the window. She didn't seem that interested in the conversation. I wondered why. I knew Elena Maria's *quinceañera* was very important to her.

The River Walk was right on the San Antonio River. We walked along paths shaded by flowering trees and plants. This led us to the back entrances of many of the mall's shops, which was a picturesque route. Luckily there were plenty of ramps for wheelchairs. Aunt Lourdes and I took turns pushing Mom from store to store. Mom dubbed us her "escorts."

The grown-ups and Elena Maria seemed to delight in

the endless search for the right shoes. Lauren and Jill were happy to discuss the benefits of silk versus satin as well. I was losing interest fast.

"I'm so in love," Lauren sighed. "Tony! What a dreamboat. How does such a hot dude have such a funny-looking little brother like Ricardo?" I suddenly felt protective of Rico and his goofy glasses and big ears.

"He's very smart," I said a little defensively.

"Alfonso's just fine with me," Jill said. "With his long curly hair, he reminds me of a rock star."

I was getting tired of tagging along behind Lauren and Jill. They had nothing to talk about but boys—except when they argued about whether my sister should wear pink (Jill) or white (Lauren).

As Elena Maria tried on shoe after shoe, I got that familiar ants-in-my-pants feeling. Then I had an idea. On the way in we had passed by a gallery with an interesting name—the Blue Turtle.

I tapped my mother a couple of times on her shoulder. "What is it, Isabel?" she finally asked, sounding impatient, as she was trying to pay attention to my sister's questions.

"Can I go outside? I want to see the art gallery on the River Walk."

Elena Maria had the three adults' attention firmly in hand. She was arguing the finer points of spaghetti straps versus a princess neckline. Katani would have loved the conversation, but I was ready to leave. Mom nodded without looking at me, but that was all the permission I needed.

I was outside in a flash, skipping down the River Walk, on the lookout for the Blue Turtle Art Gallery. Who wouldn't want to walk into a gallery called the Blue Turtle?

It wasn't far, just four doors down. I came upon stone entrance steps and was enchanted by what I saw through the massive glass doors. I walked in. The front gallery was filled with bronze statues of all kinds of animals. I circled one of a buffalo that looked so lifelike I wanted to reach out and touch it. Having just made that huge mistake, I kept my hands in my pockets and began walking around in the rest of the gallery.

I approached a large figure of a woman's head. I could not make out her expression. Was she asleep, or half-awake? In pain, or full of happiness?

"Ah," said a deep voice behind me. "*La Llorona* exerts a power over all who enter here, whether they're eight years old or eighty." I turned to see a very tall man dressed in jeans and a leather vest, his dark hair plaited into two long, shiny braids. He extended a hand encrusted with silver and turquoise rings and bracelets.

"*Daaaaaad,*" said a voice from behind him. I peeked around his imposing figure and saw a girl a little older than me, maybe fourteen, running into the shop through a big sliding-glass door. Behind her, in a courtyard sort of area, was a potter's wheel and all sorts of half-formed sculptures and pots.

The girl gracefully slid around her dad and stopped in front of him, facing me. She had black hair like his, except that hers was supershort and spiky, some of it tipped in

"I came upon stone entrance steps
and was entranced by what I saw ... "

green. "You don't have to listen to him being all dramatic," she told me, rolling her eyes. Behind her, I could see her dad smiling. "*La Llorona* means 'the weeping woman.' Do you like art?"

Whoa. With her awesomely wild hair and straight-forward style, this girl was a lot to take in all at once. She was kind of a teenage, Western version of Razzberry Pink, the proprietor of Think Pink, my friend Maeve's favorite store in all of Boston. "Um, yeah," I finally answered softly.

Her dad put an arm around her shoulder. "My name is Cesar Arnoldo Guerrero, proprietor of this most humble gallery, and creator, I'm afraid, of this mysterious piece that everybody can't get enough of, but nobody ever buys."

His impatient daughter rolled her eyes again and said, "Dad, that's because people don't like to have sad things around their house."

"Yes, TV says you must be happy all the time or you are a big loser, right?" he answered with a smile.

I was starting to like Mr. Guerrero. He was funny and his eyes looked kind, and when he spoke I felt a little braver. I finally found my voice to compliment him on the beautiful sculpture. "This is really cool! How do you make this?"

"Metal, fire, and a little bit of magic. An artist, like a good magician, never gives away his secrets."

"Magicians tell other magicians how they do their tricks, if they think they're good enough," his daughter countered. This girl was very direct and definitely not the artsy-sensitive type. Mr. Guerrero laughed a big, hearty laugh. "That's true, daughter. But we don't know yet if our visitor is one of us—an artist." He looked at me with questioning eyes.

"I am," I said boldly.

"I knew it!" the girl cried, clapping her hands together. "I could just tell from the way you were looking at *La Llorona*. Like you were really studying it, really seeing the art, you know?"

I blushed and nodded. She knew I was an artist just from the way I looked at art? What a compliment!

"I'm Xochitl," she told me. "That's Zooooo-cheeeeel, but it's spelled x-o-c-h-i-t-l. People always get it wrong. Anyway, what's your name?"

"Isabel."

"Nice to meet a fellow artist," Mr. Guerrero said and shook my hand.

As the three of us walked along, he pointed to some of the paintings and told me the artists' names and where they were from. Xochitl was constantly jumping in to add some funny detail. Mr. Guerrero didn't seem to mind, though. Xochitl really did know a lot about the art. I was so impressed that someone who was not much older than me was so knowledgeable about art. I guessed that living and breathing art every day was like taking an art vitamin pill every morning of your life.

"Here at the Blue Turtle Gallery we celebrate the culture of our ancestors," he explained, as we arrived back at *La Llorona*. "Our family, for example, is of Coahuilteca-Apache lineage. Of course we're Mexican, too."

"My name means 'flower' in Nahuatl, the old Aztec language," Xochitl interjected.

"Oh, wow! It sounds so pretty, too. And your last name, Guerrero, means warrior, right?" I was proud that I remembered the English translation.

"Yes. But trust me, we're a very peace-loving family."

Mr. Guerrero made me laugh, and I was beginning to relax in his presence. "My cousin was talking about the Coah-whoa-whoa-whatevers last night," I told them.

Xochitl laughed and shook her head. "Kwo-weel-tek-ah," she said slowly.

"Right," I answered, laughing too. "Sorry. I'll learn to pronounce it eventually. But Apache . . . I've heard that they were fierce warriors, weren't they?"

Mr. Guerrero smiled again. "Not all the time. But even up to the nineteenth century, San Antonians still had to be on the lookout. People still find arrowheads out there, outside the city."

I thought about what a thrill it would be to find a genuine arrowhead on my cousins' ranch. As I looked around the gallery again, my eyes returned to the statue of the mysterious woman—*La Llorona*. "I'd love to learn to do metalwork like that someday," I said, gazing at the rich luster of the bronze.

"No way!" Xochitl exclaimed. "Isabel, I was working on a model for a bronze casting out in the courtyard when you came in! Can I show her, Dad?"

"Of course," Mr. Guerrero agreed. "I need to get back to some bookkeeping up here at the desk. But I'm certain

Xochitl can give you just as good a tour of our studio space as I could."

"Better, actually," Xochitl teased. "Come on!"

I thought about this. I wasn't sure how long I had been in the gallery, and I wondered if my family was looking for me. On the other hand . . . a real artist's studio space! And Elena Maria probably wouldn't be done dress shopping for *hours*. "I guess so," I said finally. "But I really should get back soon."

"Sure, sure," Xochitl said, pulling me out the back door. "This is so cool, you're going to love it!" She led me over to an old wooden worktable, covered in layers of paint splatters. Right in the middle was a large clay model of a bird.

"I'm trying to sculpt a heron, but something about it is just not right. I just can't *see* what's wrong with it. It's driving me crazy."

"You like birds?" I asked.

"Love, love them," she answered.

I told her all about my bird cartoons. "Wow, that's so cool," she responded when I was done. "What do you think of my heron? I know there is something off, but I'm not sure what."

I walked around and around, checking out her piece, and then it struck me. "I think I know why it seems off to you. This part, the curve from the head to the back at the neck . . . I think maybe it's a touch too short. Try making the head a little rounder and the neck a little longer," I suggested, looking up at Xochitl. I hoped I didn't sound like too much of a know-it-all. I really liked her and hoped we could be friends.

She walked around her bird, looking at it from different angles. I had a sudden fear that maybe she was insulted by what I had said. But she burst out with, "You're right, you're absolutely right, Isabel." She slapped a glop of red clay on the back of the head and began to mold. She stepped back. "That's it. Genius, Isabel. I can't thank you enough."

I blushed. "I like to draw birds. They're so . . . birdlike." Xochitl cracked up at that one.

"You have an awesome sense of dimension," she said. "Would you like to work on something? Come on, don't be shy." Xochitl tossed me a small brick of pottery clay. Before I knew it I was kneading and pinching the clay. It turned soft in my hands. In a matter of minutes I shaped a small parrot.

"That's so cute," Xochitl said, striking a pose with a hand under her chin. "It's so parrotlike," she joked.

"I don't think I got the feet right, though. The feet on your heron look better proportioned. My parrot has too-tiny feet!"

We were in the middle of an intense bird-feet discussion—with some high octane laughing, because Xochitl decided to mimic a heron walking in high heels—when the door to the courtyard slid open. Mr. Guerrero and a policeman entered.

"Miss Martinez?"

"Yes, officer," I answered. My heart was pounding

like a huge grandfather clock in my chest. Had the broken eagle been discovered?

"Young woman, you've caused quite a scare to your family," he said. Almost immediately, the entire shopping gang appeared behind him: Lauren and Jill looked giddy from shopping but annoyed, and so did Elena Maria, Aunt Lourdes, who wheeled in my mother, and Aunt Inez, who towered over me.

"*¡Muchachita! Dios mío*, we were so scared. I was worried you were kidnapped," Aunt Inez said, putting her hands to her throat. "Don't *ever* leave again without asking us permission."

I was so embarrassed. "I-I-I'm sorry, Aunt Inez. I told Mom—"

"Isabel, you completely disappeared on me," my mother said.

"No, I didn't. I told you—"

Aunt Lourdes interrupted. "Do not contradict your mother. You've caused enough of a stir."

"Lourdes, enough," my mother defended me. "We have found our Isabel. The search party has been successful." I gave her a huge smile. Having three mothers was two too many for me.

"Hold on a minute," Xochitl said. "Isabel, Mrs. Ruiz is your aunt?"

"Yeah," I said. "You know my family?"

"Of course," Mr. Guerrero agreed. "The Ruizes are great patrons of this gallery. They practically keep us in business some years!" He smiled kindly at Aunt Inez.

My stomach began the butterfly dance as I held my breath. I did a quick scan of the gallery through the sliding glass doors, but I didn't see any glass sculpture. I let my breath out slowly. My aunt must buy from several artists in San Antonio, I reassured myself.

"When I saw your appreciation for *La Llorona*, Isabel," Mr. Guerrero went on, "I should have known you were a member of this family."

I didn't know what to say. I simply stood there, terribly ashamed about causing such a big scene. Xochitl put her hand on my elbow. "Isabel, let me fire your statue. It looks pretty finished to me."

Aunt Inez spoke up. "Thank you for your offer," she said to Xochitl. "I can pick it up later or it can be delivered to my home." She turned to Mr. Guerrero. "Cesar, thank God she was in good hands. I'm not used to girls," she said, twisting her ring.

"She was never in any danger, Inez. Perhaps she could have been a little clearer when she separated from you." He turned and gave me a wink, but it didn't make me feel any better.

I waved good-bye to Xochitl and followed everybody out of the courtyard. When we were back on the River Walk, Elena Maria grabbed my by the arm and chewed me out. "Mami nearly had a heart attack, Izzy. *Please* act more mature."

Urggg! "*Me* act more mature? Elena, you're the one who just spent a whole morning deciding between pink or white shoes!"

"That's an important decision, *mi hermanita*," Elena Maria said condescendingly. "You'll understand when you're older." She exchanged all-knowing glances with Jill and Lauren.

I ran to catch up with my mother and Aunt Lourdes, but as soon as I got there, a voice cried out "Lourdes!" We all turned around to see a woman hurrying toward our group.

"Julia! Oh my goodness!" Aunt Lourdes exclaimed, sounding surprised and happy.

"I can't believe it!" the woman went on as she reached us and gave Aunt Lourdes a big hug. "It's really a small world, isn't it? What are you doing in San Antonio?"

As they chatted I apologized again to Mom. "I'm sorry, Mami, I really am. I thought you heard me when I said I was going to the art gallery."

"Honey, there are a hundred art galleries along the River Walk. Forget about it for now, okay? I'm just glad you're safe." She didn't sound mad at me at all. Phew.

"Are you sure?" Aunt Lourdes was saying to her friend. "It's no trouble?"

"Of course not! I would love for you to stay!"

"Well . . ." Aunt Lourdes hesitated, looking at my mom. "Esperanza, you remember Julia, from the hospital?"

"Of course," my mom replied. "It's so nice to see you again, Julia. I remember now, Lourdes told me you trans-ferred here to San Antonio."

"Julia has invited me to stay with her over these few days, Esperanza," Aunt Lourdes explained. "Of course, if you need me with you, or if *you* need me, Inez, to help out in preparation for the celebration . . . "

Aunt Inez shook her head. "It's all taken care of, Lourdes. Give us a call later and we will have your things sent on." I couldn't wait to tell the BSG about my aunt's special delivery service. It was like I was staying at Hotel Inez.

Mom agreed. "I will be just fine on my own for a few days. I have such good helpers here, after all." She smiled at Elena Maria and me.

"We can help too, Mrs. Martinez," Jill and Lauren offered.

Aunt Lourdes broke into a grin. "Wonderful! I will check in with you every day, Esperanza, Inez." She walked off talking a mile a minute with her friend, looking happier than I had seen her in ages.

But it didn't seem like Aunt Inez was ready to forgive me yet for messing up the shopping trip. She seemed really put out with me as she announced, "There is no time to dine at the Tower of the Americas restaurant. Let's return to the ranch. I'll have Fidencia and Enrique fix something for lunch."

Elena Maria was about to protest when she saw the look on my mom's face.

"I'm sorry," I whispered to Elena Maria. I did feel bad that I had ruined their lunch. Lucky for me, my sister was too excited about her purchases to be that upset.

6

Meanwhile, Back at the Ranch . . .

Elena Maria and her friends were deep in conversation with the boys, who were over-the-top excited about the missions they visited. Scott was wildly impressed by the *acequias*, the water-routing system developed by the Franciscan friars. Uncle Hector had given them a talk about the importance of water conservation. He explained that this area of Texas could experience long drought periods. And then were times when so much rain fell that entire neighborhoods would float down the river. Since I was an official member of the Green Machine, the group the BSG formed to plan our school's environmental science fair, I paid strict attention to my uncle's story.

"What's really cool about all this is that these missions were all here by the mid-seventeen-hundreds," Scott said. "Think of it! Pre–American Revolution! I always thought the thirteen original colonies had the lock on civilization in the New World."

Then Jill said something. "I did some research before we left. Did you know the Spanish had set up their government in Mexico by the middle of the fifteen hundreds?" Research? Jill of the silly iPod videos surprised me. I remembered what my friend Charlotte always said: "Be careful about judging a book by its cover. Sometimes the inside pages are full of gold."

Alfonso spoke up. "I've often wondered what this country would be like if the Spanish had succeeded in North America, instead of the British. Maybe we'd all be speaking Spanish right now."

"Oh, Fonzie," Jill said a little too adoringly. "That is something to think about." Oops! Scratch previous opinion.

Ricardo and I sat at the farthest end of the long table. My cousin choked down a laugh, then crossed his eyes just as I took a big gulp of milk. It went flying, out of my nose, my mouth, everywhere.

Ricardo totally cracked up.

"Good one, Izzy," Scott exclaimed, obviously impressed.

"Thanks, Scott," I said gratefully. I looked over at Elena Maria.

"Oh, Izzy!" My sister got up and wiped the tabletop clean with my napkin as if I were a six-year-old and couldn't do it myself.

Frustrated with my sister's "I'm more mature than

you" attitude, I picked up my plate and my glass and walked into the kitchen with my head held high. I heard Elena Maria say, "Guys, I'm going to get some more milk."

She marched into the kitchen after me and began scolding. "Why are you embarrassing me? I'm trying to give my friends an unforgettable time. It's so obvious you need attention, just like a little baby."

I crossed my arms and frowned. "Well, if I'm such a baby, why am I the only one who gets her own room?"

"Well, if you think you're all grown-up, then here," she said, handing me a camera. "Play photographer and document our fun times." She left the kitchen skipping.

Hello? Why was Elena acting so different? I promised myself that I would never change when I became a teenager.

Enrique and Fidencia, the two cooks, whispered to each other. He took a mug from a cabinet and handed it to his wife, who ladled something that smelled sweet and familiar into it. Hot chocolate!

"*Toma*," he said, placing it before me. Drink it.

"*Gracias*, Enrique, Fidencia. *Me gusta mucho el chocolate.*" All the BSG were crazy about hot chocolate, including me.

The two cooks were thrilled to hear me speak an entire sentence in Spanish. They peppered me with questions about school, my father, which boy was Elena Maria's *chambelan de honor*, and whether I had a boyfriend.

"I'm only twelve," I said in my best Spanish accent. "I don't have a real boyfriend yet."

Enrique said something I couldn't make out for sure, but I know it was like, "Your mother will be fighting off boys with a broom." I blushed hotly, which sent Fidencia into a fit of laughter, and me out of the kitchen.

It was late in the day, but the sun was far from setting. I took in a breath, heard a bird chirp, and felt the warm sun on my arms. The older kids and my cousins (except Ricardo) were in the swimming pool, flirting and playing ball. Tony and Alfonso had invited some friends over too. A radio blasted hip-hop and rock and roll, but nobody cared or complained. Even though we were close to the city we were in the middle of nowhere, surrounded by hills.

I wondered what Ricardo was up to, even though I was still upset with him for our incident with the eagle statue the night before. My sister and her friends were busy, and every time I played paparazzi, which my sister had asked me to do, one of them would complain.

"No, Izzy. My hair's not right," Lauren said.

"Izzy, seriously, please don't take pictures of me at that angle," Jill said. "It makes me look fat." Jill looked like she weighed about ten pounds. I decided then and there that I would never be one of those girls who complains all the time about being fat, especially if I was skinny. It's so annoying.

At one point I asked Tony and his friends to bunch together, which they seemed happy to do, but Elena Maria scolded me. "Izzy, can't you be like real paparazzi? Hide in the bushes and shoot from there or something. You know, so we have candids."

Everybody found this incredibly funny. I did not. I walked away thinking, *Take your own pictures, Elena Maria.* Where was my sister? The one who cooked for me, who helped me with my hair, laughed with me. Where was that sister? I missed her.

It was dark and cool inside the house. The doors to the living room were closed, thank goodness. Maybe nobody had discovered anything yet. I decided to go see my mother and went to her room, expecting to find her there, but it was empty. I ran into Mercedes, who was mopping.

"*Dónde está mi mamá?*" I asked.

"*En el balcón,*" she said, pointing upstairs.

Sure enough, I found her on an ancient rocking chair, looking out at the horizon. I gave her a kiss on the cheek and then leaned over the railing and took in the beautiful view. A few dark clouds were visible over a range of hills, but there were blue skies above us. It was an Isabel Martinez kind of day—except for my sister and her friends.

"That must be the start of the Hill Country that Tony was talking about," I said.

Mom touched my hand. Holding it, I grabbed a nearby stool and sat next to her. We sat in silence, feeling a lovely breeze on our cheeks, listening to the birds that shrieked in the distance. I could have done this forever, except a cow let out this gigantic moo, and that got us both laughing.

"Boy, Mami, this place is beautiful. You should see my room. It's got white walls, but the color changes by the hour with the sunlight. I didn't want to be there at first because it was so far away from everybody else, but now I love it. It's *charming*," I said, waving my arms around, mimicking Aunt Inez. Mom gave me a funny look.

"I'll go take a look later, my dear. Right now I just want to sit here and rest. There's nothing for me to do. Inez has taken care of every little detail," she said, sounding a little wistful.

"I think she's just trying to be nice, Mom." I worried that Mom didn't laugh at my imitation of Aunt Inez.

"I know that, but . . ."

"I know what you mean. Even Ricardo said last night his mom was a little pushy."

Her eyebrows shot up. "He said that? What a naughty boy."

"He wasn't being mean, Mami. He just said it like it was a fact."

My mother shook her head. "Poor, poor Inez. All the money in the world can't give her what she really wants. A daughter."

"But Mom, she has so much. Have you seen the artwork in the living room? It's . . ." I suddenly realized what I was saying and stopped myself. The last thing I wanted to talk about was the art collection.

"It's beautiful, *sí*?" She finished the sentence for me. I nodded silently. "Yes, I heard about that magnificent art collection downstairs. What a blessing to afford such fine things." She paused. "Perhaps I should go and look at this fine collection everyone is talking about. Would you like to take me on a little tour, Isabel?"

My heart was pounding. I thought fast. "Um, I would, but . . . it's so nice just sitting out here, don't you think?"

My mom smiled. "That is true. This landscape in front of us is just as lovely as any painting, and being here with you makes me much happier than any piece of artwork ever could."

I felt my heart returning to a normal rhythm, but I also felt completely terrible. I wanted to tell Mom everything. How Ricardo and I were in the living room when we weren't supposed to be, how we broke the tip off the eagle's wing. I opened my mouth but closed it again quickly. Mom looked so happy staring out at the hills, I just couldn't upset her. Later. I would tell her later. I formulated a plan that I would tell her after the *quince* was over. Maybe just before we left for the airport.

"Ricardo said they're not rich, they're just lucky," I told her.

She shifted in her seat. "Yes, the Ruiz family has been lucky indeed. Just look at this view. I would love to have even a *ranchito* someday."

"When I'm a famous artist, I'll buy you one. We'll call it Bluebird Ranch, after the Bluebird of Happiness." She squeezed my hand tighter, and we continued to look at the sky and the hills.

"You know what I think? I think I am the luckiest woman in the world. I have the best family that anyone could ask for. My two girls are more valuable than any piece of art, or piece of dirt, or herd of cattle, cook staff, cleaning lady . . ." She looked at me with a guilty smile.

"Mami? Are you a little bit jealous?" I teased.

"Ah, you are perceptive, my little Isabel. Okay, maybe I could use a housekeeper every now and then." She patted my back. "Now, *mi 'jita*, come with me. I want to show you something. It's a secret we must keep from your sister."

I was intrigued and wondered what my mom had up her sleeve now. Back in her room, Mom reached into the closet and withdrew a small box. She placed it on a desk and opened it.

"Oh! What's all this, Mami?"

She put a paper figure on a desk. It was an origami-style cat, made from yellow paper with brown and black spots. "This is a jaguar." She brought out a few more. "And this is a dove. Here is an elephant, a swan, a monkey, a deer, a snake."

I recognized the rest: a bear, a whale, a mouse, a dog, an owl, a duck, a lamb, a cow, and a unicorn. Each was made with printed paper to resemble the animal's skin.

"Are these party favors?" I asked.

"Yes, I've made almost a hundred of these."

"Mami, no!"

"Yes, Mami, *sí*!" She laughed.

"When did you do all this? How long have you been doing origami? These are beautiful."

"I used to do this in college, especially when I needed a break from my exams. I've been making these for Elena Maria's *quinceañera* while you girls were at school."

She'd been preparing for Elena's *quince* a lot longer

than Elena thought. "These are so incredible, Mami. Wait till Elena Maria sees them."

"Shhh. I don't want you to tell her. It's a surprise."

"You don't have to worry about me, Mom," I said, pulling an imaginary zipper across my lips. She grinned and held out her arms, and I leaned over to give her giant squeeze. She held me like that for a long time. My mom was always the person who made me feel safe, and my dad always made me feel like anything was possible. At that moment, I felt like a very lucky girl, even if I didn't have a Diego Rivera painting in my living room.

"Oh, I almost forgot. There's more." Mom returned to the closet. This time she took out a large, flat folder. With her back was to me, she put it on the bed. "Look."

She'd laid out a string of colored, lacey, cut-paper sheets, each connected to the other with string. Every sheet was carefully pierced to depict a different scene. My eyes fell on a cutout of a girl in a princess gown, angels at either side: My sister, at her *quinceañera.* Another one showed a man and a woman, obviously parents, holding the hands of two little girls.

"That's us!" I cried. "*Mooooom!* You're a paper artist!" I couldn't believe it. With two hardworking accountants for parents, I'd never been able to figure out where my love of art came from. Now I knew.

"Did you know there is magic in paper, Isabel? I've been practicing *papel picado* for about a month. It was going to be my little surprise. Will you help me hang them before the celebration?"

I hopped up and twirled around. "Yes, yes, yes! This is going to be the best *quinceañera* ever, Mom. You're a star!"

"*Ay*, settle down, *muchachita*. I need to make more *animalitos*. Here is a package of paper. I'll teach you how to do it, okay? We can never have enough *animalitos* at a party, no?"

"As long as they're the paper kind, and not the obnoxious high-schooler kind," I said.

She laughed at my joke. We sat at the desk and started to work. It felt so good to be sitting there working with Mom. I decided to say something I'd been thinking for a while.

"Mami, why does Elena Maria have to be so full of herself here? It's like she doesn't even want to hear what I have to say anymore."

"Let her be, my sweet. Pretty soon she'll be a woman, so let her be a teenager. I know you feel like she's leaving you behind. But don't forget, you'll be a teenager in no time too."

She held up a sheet of paper. I copied her every time she made a new fold. She wouldn't tell me what the creature would be. I had to figure it out as we went along. Four short legs, a tiny tail, a big shell . . . a turtle! Very cool. We worked quietly, then I asked her something else I'd been wondering.

"I miss Papa. When's he getting here?"

"Dear, he will be here, I promise. Your father wouldn't miss this for the world."

If Mom and Dad were together, maybe I could tell

them about the broken eagle, and they would help me. Holding in my secret was stressing me out. I kept thinking about the eagle's wing tip, flying through my brain.

"Don't you worry, Isabel. We're going to have a wonderful, memorable family reunion this weekend." I looked at my mother's smile. It was one of those "I've-got-a-secret-and-I'm-not-going-to-tell-you" smiles. It was kind of exciting to think about what more my parents had in mind.

All of a sudden I started to giggle. "What's so funny, *mi 'jita*? Are you laughing at my little crab here?" Mom wiggled a little origami crab at me.

"No, Mami. I was just thinking . . . what if Dad drove up to the ranch in a carriage pulled by white horses, wearing a top hat and a tuxedo?"

Mom burst out laughing so hard she popped a button on her shirt. I folded the little tail on my paper turtle. Getting to hang out with my mom and dad, together, was the only family reunion I needed. Seeing all our uncles and cousins and relatives would just be icing on the giant, white, *quinceañera* cake!

CHAPTER

7

Say ¡Queso!

The patio sparkled in the evening light. Strings of bare lightbulbs danced in the wind, creating a twinkling effect. Enrique stood on a ladder, replacing a bad bulb. Mercedes put the finishing touches on the silverware, which she had spread, fanlike, next to a stack of plates and cups. Mercedes was kind of like the ranch's resident Martha Stewart. Her table settings looked amazing, like they were out of a magazine. She had placed beautiful flowers all around the table in a pattern that made you think the flowers were dancing.

Aunt Inez looked very much the hostess in a big, loose dress and a turban. She wore a lot of turquoise jewelry and her usual dramatic makeup. She definitely had star quality as she twirled through the party.

The night was perfect for outdoor dining. Half of my many relatives were there already. My grandparents on my Mom's side, Abuelito José and Abuelita Juanita, weren't getting to the ranch for a couple of days, but my father's parents, Papa Margarito and Mama Maria, and his brother's family arrived late in the afternoon. They had come all the way from Mexico! Mama Maria frightened me a little when she grabbed me by the shoulders, practically pinching me, and said: "*Cuida a tu mamá.*" Her words didn't register right away, because I realized I was now taller than her. Being taller than my grandmother must mean I was "maturing." I held my head high and smiled at my other relatives.

Mama Maria could be sort of cranky, but I loved that she had so much spirit and always said whatever she thought. She began to complain to my mom that her granddaughters were becoming "*Americanas,*" unable to hold a decent conversation in Spanish, too modern for our own good.

Papa Margarito just laughed his great, jolly laugh and said to me, "Don't worry, bay-bee. It'll be all right!" Papa was a big joker.

"*Claro que sí, Abuelo,*" I replied as I hugged them both, to prove to Mama Maria that my Spanish was just fine, thank you. She smiled and winked at me. She always said she loved *my* spirit too.

My cousin Irma, whose *quinceañera* last summer in Mexico City was still the talk of the family, arrived from Monterrey with her family. She looked so grown-up, almost like a college student, but she couldn't be older than sixteen. Her younger sister, Delia, trailed behind. She looked like she was in a mood, because she wouldn't smile at anyone. I guessed I wouldn't be hanging out with her right away.

The parade of relatives was endless. I lost track of the

connections, the second-cousin-mother's-side, my-great-aunt's-third-husband's-brother's-stepson (who invited him?), folks from Vera Cruz, some from Jalisco, somebody else from southern California. It went on and on, and it was so confusing.

All of a sudden I realized that I was surrounded by nobody I really knew, so I made my way back to Mom. She was sitting at a table with my grandparents. Mama Maria immediately started complaining about my terrible accent again. Mom just laughed it off and said in Spanish, "We live in New England. She won't forget all her Spanish. I won't let her."

Thanks, Mom, I mouthed. Suddenly Elena Maria appeared, like a butterfly. She rested her chin on her hands, which were on our grandmother's shoulder. "Hóla, Mama Maria," she sang. Their conversation was so easy that I got away from there fast.

As I looked around at all my relatives chatting away in both Spanish and English, I realized that I really had no one to blame but myself. They could all speak two languages perfectly well. I made a vow on the spot to pay more attention to Spanish at school. I mean, what if I wanted to go to art school in Mexico City someday? I'd really need to be fluent in Spanish then.

"Isabel, would you mind helping me to bed?" Mom asked me. "It's been a long day. I think the wheelchair is just over in that corner."

I ran to get it and brought it back to the table, then helped my mom stand up and sit back down in it. "Good night, Maria, Margarito," she said politely. "I hope you'll excuse me for turning in early tonight."

"Of course," Mama Maria said to her in Spanish, very seriously. "You must take care of yourself, Esperanza."

After I got Mom all tucked in, I headed back out to the party. All those people, laughing and chattering away . . . but it seemed like no one wanted to talk to me. I spotted Elena Maria and her friends in a cluster at the pool. Elena Maria and Scott stood by the diving board, away from the others. Poolside romance? I had to get closer and see what was going on there. Avery was going to need a Scott and Elena Maria romance update.

I sneaked alongside the wall of the house and scooted like a rabbit to the long hedge that bordered one side of the pool. Duckwalking, I waddled close to where they were all splashing around in the shallow end. I felt a little sorry for myself as I watched them. Everyone was having a great time except me.

When Scott and Elena Maria rejoined the group, I had a brilliant idea. This was going to be so funny. I decided to do what she asked and play a real paparazzo. I grabbed Elena's camera out of my purse, and just when her posse was about to walk by me, I sprang from the bushes and shouted "Surprise!" while snapping photos in rapid succession.

I was greeted by shrieks. "Isabel! What are you doing?" Jill screeched.

I continued to snap away. "Smile, Elena Maria," I yelled.

"Isabel! Give me that camera!" my shocked sister demanded.

I moved the camera out of her reach, behind my back. "But, Elena, you told me to play paparazzi!" I said. In my heart I knew I was being Isabel the pest, but I couldn't seem to control myself.

"Give me that camera!" she pleaded as she tapped her hands against her thighs.

I shook my head and Elena Maria turned away. Scott followed her.

Jill spoke first, very coolly. "Chill out somewhere else, little sister. Go."

"Yeah, Izzy. Elena's pretty mad at you right now," Lauren said.

Now I felt really bad. All I had really wanted was for Elena to pay attention to me. "I'm sorry, everybody. Really. I didn't mean to bother you. I just thought you would think it was funny."

Andy cracked up. "Actually, Isabel, you were kind of funny." Lauren's and Jill's eyes burned holes in him.

The two girls spun around and ran off after Elena Maria. Andy gave me a sympathetic look and then took off behind them.

On my way back to the patio, I passed Aunt Inez walking out of the kitchen with another tall, thin woman, who was wearing just as much makeup and jewelry. Must be another cousin or something, I figured. They were carrying huge trays of steaming enchiladas and talking very seriously. I quickly ducked behind a big oak tree to let them pass me. I was still feeling a little shy around Aunt Inez.

"That is just terrible! Such beautiful work," the tall, thin woman was saying as they walked by.

"I know," Aunt Inez answered sadly. "I discovered it this morning. That piece means so much to me. Such incredible craftsmanship . . . and now it's broken."

My legs began to wobble and my breath got shallow.

"Do you know who is responsible?" the other woman asked.

"Oh," Aunt Inez replied, lowering her voice. I strained to hear. "I have an idea, but no one seems to have seen the accident, and I don't want to start making accusations without any proof. . . ."

I couldn't make out the rest, but that was enough. My heart was pounding. She knew the eagle was broken. Did she know it was me and Ricardo who broke it? I had to talk to Ricardo. *Now.*

I starting running around the barbecue like a crazy person, darting in and out of the crowd as I searched everywhere for him. Of course he would disappear at a time like this! *Ricardo, Ricardo, where are you?* I repeated to myself, getting more and more upset. *Where is that boy?*

Finally I spotted him creeping along the back fence, looking back over his shoulder every couple of steps. Definitely suspicious. What was he doing now? I didn't have time to worry about that at the moment, though. I ran up behind him and grabbed his arm. "Ricardo!" I yelled, out of breath.

"Whoa!" he jumped practically a mile in the air, then turned bright red. "Oh, uh, hey, Isabel. I didn't hear you."

"Ricardo, listen, we are in trouble. Serious trouble. Your mom knows about the eagle!"

He went pale. "Sh-sh-she does?" he stuttered. "She knows we broke it?"

"Yes!" I cried. Then I thought for a second. "Well, she knows it's broken. I just heard her telling another of our aunts about it. She said she's not sure who did it."

"Well, she didn't name you and me, specifically," he pressed.

"Umm . . . well . . . she said she didn't have any proof."

Ricardo frowned and thought for a second. "I wonder how long she's known about it. . . ."

"Oh, I did hear that," I offered. "She said she found it this morning."

"Ah-ha!" he cried. "That's the proof. We're totally off the hook for this."

"What? Why?"

"Isabel, check it out. If she found out this morning, and she definitely knows it was us who did it, don't you think she would have said something to us by now? I mean, this is my mother."

"Well . . . you do have a point." We both knew Aunt Inez was not the type to let something like this slide. I could feel my heart starting to slow down to normal speed again. Maybe we weren't in gigantically huge trouble after all. "Okay," I finally agreed. "You're probably right."

"I'm definitely right," he told me, nodding. But I had a funny feeling he was really trying convince himself that he was right, not me.

"So . . . what are you doing over here by yourself, anyway?" I asked him.

"Uhhh, nothing," he answered quickly.

Now, I knew *that* wasn't true. "Uh-huh," I said. "That's why you were acting all suspicious right before I got over here, right? I saw you."

He looked at me guiltily and pushed up his thick glasses. "You have to promise not to tell," he warned.

"No way. I'm not promising anything until you tell me what's up."

He considered this, then leaned in. "Okay. I'm going out to look for armadillos."

"Armadillos? Do they bite?"

Ricardo laughed. "No. They're harmless, like little scaredy-cats. Just don't get too close. They carry fleas."

"I won't get too close."

"What? You want to come?"

"Yes! Please?" Chasing armadillos sounded much better than sitting around here all night waiting for the bomb to drop. Maybe the armadillos would even talk to me. Now *that* would be funny.

Ricardo became animated. "Follow me to my room. Let me get my boots." He looked at my sneakers. "Did you bring any boots?"

"No. What do I need boots for?"

He gave me a dumb, empty look. "For the horse?"

"The *what*?" It dawned on me. "We're going to look for armadillos on horseback?"

He pushed his glasses up his nose and nodded rapidly. "Boots work better than sneakers."

"Whoa, wait a minute. I don't know how to ride a horse. I've never even been on a horse."

"Piece of cake. I can loan you some boots. Come on."

No Horsing Around

To tell you the truth, I was kind of surprised by Ricardo's bedroom. It was pretty big and it was very neat for a boy, except for the scads of books and CDs everywhere. I looked around while he searched his closet for boots. One wall had a bunch of different maps—some old, some modern, and some with squiggly green lines. He had lots of rodeo posters and photos. I saw a framed picture of a small boy wrestling a calf to the ground, wrapping a rope around its legs. This same kid was in another photo, this time on a horse, roping a steer.

"Ricardo, is this you?" I asked.

He emerged from the closet, holding a fine-looking leather bag. "Yeah, that's me. I came in third, though."

I would have asked him more, but I saw something in a corner that stopped me cold. A great, big, red accordion, splayed open on a chair as if it had recently been played.

"Is *that* yours?"

He nodded proudly. "I got that for my birthday last year. It's a classic."

I closed in for a better look. I'd never seen one of these

instruments up so close before. It was beautiful. The red lacquer on the box shined to infinity. The keyboard was nothing compared to the row of a million buttons beside it.

"Can I touch it?" I asked, pointing to the sharp pleats in the bellows.

"Sure!"

I ran my finger down the crease of one of the folds. Paper. Nice! I spun to face him. "What's that music I've been hearing for days now? It's everywhere. The one with accordions. It sounds like German music but the singing is in Spanish."

"You meant conjunto?"

"Is that what it's called? It's really neat. Is it old-fashioned Mexican music?"

"Actually, it's kind of Mexican-*American* music. It started in the fields and on farms a long time ago, then San Antonio became a major recording center in the early twentieth century for Spanish music. *Conjunto* just means 'ensemble' in Spanish. And you're right on about the German influence. They brought the accordion to these parts." Ricardo was smiling and talking quickly. I hadn't seen him get so excited about anything since we arrived.

"And you can play this?" I started to see Ricardo in a very different light. He was like one of the Renaissance people you read about in history books.

"I've been taking classes for a while," he said proudly. "I'm a member of the Conjunto Heritage *Taller. Taller* means 'workshop.' It's a center in San Antonio where *everybody* goes to learn. I'll burn you a CD so you can take it home with you, if you want."

"That's so nice. Thanks, Rico."

"Here are some old boots for you . . . I think they'll fit. Let's get going. I've got to saddle up Rasquatch. It won't take long."

I gulped. "Does Rasquatch bite?"

"Yes. And if you're not careful, he'll step on you too." Then he laughed. "Just kidding," he said when he saw my expression.

Down by the stable, I waited in the dark. Ricardo finally showed up, leading Rasquatch by the reins.

"I was going to lend you your own horse, but since you don't know how to ride . . ."

Uh-oh. I knew what he meant. "We have to ride one horse together?"

In the blink of an eye he was up on the horse. "Well, come on already."

My feet were glued to the ground. Ricardo held out his hand.

I had to confess. "What am I supposed to do?"

He dismounted, and stood close to me. He connected his hands like a bridge and held them out. I had no idea what he was doing. He changed his stance.

"Let's try something else. Isabel, you've got to get on the horse, so listen up. Stand there, hold the horn here with your left hand, put your left foot into the stirrup, and at the same time liiiiiift your right leg and swing it over the saddle and sit down."

I put my foot in the stirrup but managed only to bob up and down a few times. "I can't do it!" I cried. "This horse is too high."

"Yes, you can. You just can't think about it too much. Look, it's easy. Just watch me do it."

He got up on the horse again. He made it look so easy.

"Yee-haw!" I wisecracked, and suddenly I was right up behind him. Well, Ricardo grabbed me by the arm to help. But mostly it was me.

"Good job, Isabel. You ready?"

CHAPTER

8

Armadillos About

As soon as I landed on the saddle, the horse bucked forward and whinnied. I instinctively tightened my grip around Ricardo.

"Whoa, whoa, Rasquatch! Down, boy." At Ricardo's voice, the skittish horse calmed. We trotted into the darkening night.

The sounds of the party receded. In a short while I was enjoying myself tremendously. We covered a lot of ground quickly. Ricardo did not bring the horse to a stop until we'd ridden for at least a quarter of an hour.

"Are we still on the ranch?" I asked nervously. I didn't want to get into any more trouble.

"Oh, yeah, and this is usually a good place to find armadillos," he said. "Okay, watch me dismount and do the same thing." He hopped off the horse, and I slid down after him.

Ricardo rummaged through the leather sack he'd attached to the saddle. He withdrew a flashlight and handed it to me. Next he pulled out an old-style canteen. He made a big show of unscrewing the cap and taking a big swig. He offered it to me. I laughed, feeling like Ricardo and I were in *Raiders of the Lost Ark*.

"Will you pass me the flashlight, please?" he asked.

I wordlessly handed it to him. He pointed it toward the ground and turned it on. He took a few steps in one direction, then the other. "I always see 'dillos around here. There's a nest somewhere nearby. But I don't even see tracks tonight."

I sighed loudly and stared at the ground. It all just looked like dirt and rocks and grass to me. Then something caught my eye. Something moving.

"Over here!" I shouted. Ricardo shined the light where I was pointing . . . just in time for us to see a long, gray, ringed tail disappear into the weeds.

"Aw, Isabel, you scared the critter away!" Ricardo groaned. "You gotta be quiet if you want an armadillo to come out. They're very shy."

"Sorry, Ricardo," I apologized, "but this *is* my first time looking for armadillos."

We stood there for another five or ten minutes saying absolutely nothing while Ricardo swept the flashlight back and forth over the ground. Suddenly I heard a low rumbling noise. Thunder boomed somewhere far away.

Finally Ricardo gave up. "I've got an idea. Let's go see the *tinaja*. The water's deep right now. It's been raining. And I can show you something really cool!"

I was excited to see the old swimming hole. I did a little dance and said, "Let's go, cowboy!"

"Isabel," Ricardo said, "you are a funny *chica*." In a minute we were back in the saddle, and we reached the base of the hills in no time.

We dismounted, and I looked around and clapped my hands in delight. Here it was, the very place that in my memories was forever magical. The *tinaja* was just beyond those trees, a little higher up. I couldn't wait to see the rock overhang that sometimes had water running over it.

"I've got to see this again in the daytime," I said. "Can we come back here tomorrow?" Ricardo hung his head.

"Please?"

"You know something, I'm not supposed to be here. I can get into big trouble if my father finds out I've come here. Especially at night."

"What? Ricardo, what's the matter with you? First the living room, now this. It's like you're trying to get us in trouble."

"You wanted to see it."

"I know, but I didn't know that your father doesn't want you coming out here."

Ricardo wouldn't look me in the eye. "Well, I do have something I want to show you. It's right beyond the *tinaja*, further up the hill." He pushed his glasses up his nose and started up the hill, leading the horse by the reins.

"So what is it?" I asked, following him.

He finally looked back at me. "It's a cave. I discovered it a year ago."

"A cave? Isn't that kind of dangerous?" But the wind was blustery and cool, and he didn't hear my question.

After a few more steps, Ricardo stopped. I ran past him to the top of the low rise. Below me lay a pool of black water, sharply outlined against the limestone bowl that contained it. The rock wall that formed a half-dome over the pool was every bit as impressive as I remembered. It almost felt like we were the first humans to find the pool.

I tried to recall how it felt to splash in the water, but it had been so long. I could absolutely see why I thought of this place as a hangout for fairy tea parties. There was something magical about it.

Ricardo tied the horse's reins to a tree. He got the flashlight and walked past me. "Come on. The cave is right up here. Let's make this fast."

We climbed up a gravelly path. My foot slid on loose rocks. I grabbed a tree branch and to save myself from falling down.

"Ouch!"

"You okay?"

"Yes. We have to be careful. I hurt my knee one time, back when I took ballet. How much farther?" I asked, out of breath.

"We're almost there. It's not steep. Just watch out for the moss," he warned.

A few more steps, and both of us landed on level ground. The flashlight went out and I jumped at the darkness. Ricardo hit it against his palm a few times. It switched on. The wind whipped up and flying sand zapped me in the eyes.

"Ow!"

"Sorry, this way," Ricardo apologized, holding out his hand to help me climb some more. He aimed the flashlight at a stone wall. A jagged black opening was visible. To me, this did not look inviting.

He had that look again, the same one he'd had when he talked about his accordion—a smile from ear to ear. His glasses had fallen down his nose again. I could see his eyes, which were big and brown. I hadn't really noticed them before.

"No."

"Yes."

"You've got to be kidding. I am not going in there."

"Are you afraid? Don't be, Isabel. We'll only go in a few feet. I've got a flashlight. Please . . . you'll love it in there."

"Well, okay," I said, hesitating. "But let's hurry up. It's getting spooky out here."

Suddenly I remembered Aunt Inez's voice telling me never to leave without asking permission. I just kind of forgot. Hunting armadillos just seemed so interesting.

Rico wasted no time. I had to scramble to stay near him . . . and near the flashlight. When we got to the entrance, Ricardo kept close to the opening. He waved the flashlight over the walls with slow, controlled movements. But he seemed more interested in the floor.

"How deep is this cave?" I asked.

"I don't know. I've never been in here before. I actually just found it last week," he explained sheepishly.

"You've never—but you said—" Before I could ask if he was crazy, a sound like the sky splitting apart shook me to my bones. I heard the horse whinny from outside the cave. The thunderclap boomed for what seemed like an entire minute. We stood stock-still, each of our mouths in a frozen "Oh!" It finally ended.

"Rasquatch!" Ricardo cried. He ran to the cave entrance. "Rats! There he goes. He's off," he said.

As if on cue, the rain started. I heard it pound the ground outside. Its intensity frightened me. "Who's off?" I asked.

"Who do you think? Rasquatch."

"The horse is gone!"

"Well, it's raining too hard now to see. But my guess is yes. The good thing is that horses know their way home. He'll head towards the barn."

"The good thing?" I couldn't believe my ears. And was Ricardo's voice shaking? An icy chill ran through me from head to toe. I thought I would faint. Lightning struck and illuminated the sheet of rain. I could not take my eyes off the cave entrance. Another crack of lightning was so sharp and sounded so near that I flinched.

Ricardo stayed at the entrance. Unbelievably, the rain fell even harder.

"What are we going to do?" I asked.

"Wait."

"Wait for what? For the horse to come back?" My voice sounded shaky to my ears.

"Are you kidding? That horse isn't coming back. I meant, wait for the rain to end." Ricardo's sudden calmness irritated me. We were silent for a moment. Then he said, "And . . . one more thing. This is the season for flash floods. If this storm is one of those, then we might be stuck here for a while."

"For a while! How long, Ricardo?"

He thought about this. "Mmm, till the morning, maybe. Sunup, probably." I wanted to strangle him. My cousin had a few scrambled eggs in his brain as far as I was concerned.

The rain sounded a long way from easing up. Every so often the lightning flashed and thunder would follow, not as menacing as before, but just as powerful. Endless minutes passed. My stomach erupted in a long, drawn-out snarl. I started to laugh nervously. So did Ricardo.

"Jeez, Isabel! What are you, a bear?" he said.

I cracked up. Ricardo's funky sense of humor made me feel a little better.

Suddenly there was another crack of thunder. Without an explanation, Ricardo shut off the flashlight.

"Hey!" I shouted.

"Sorry," he muttered. "Gotta save the battery."

Every time lightning flashed I saw clear as day that our situation was still the same. The rain was coming down hard. I thought about our predicament. We didn't even ask permission to leave the party. Worse, I worried that me being lost in a storm would aggravate my mother's MS.

I rested my head on my knees and thought about how messed up everything had become, at what was supposed to be a beautiful time for my family. It was like the Bluebird of Happiness decided to take a vacation or something.

CHAPTER
9
A Cave of Mysteries

Neither Ricardo nor I had a watch, so it was impossible to say how long we'd been stuck in the cave. Ricardo was too quiet. Maybe he was scared too. I really wished the BSG were here. No matter what, we would have kept up a chat just to keep the heebie-jeebies away.

The rain lightened up occasionally, but as soon as our spirits lifted, the clouds tricked us and ripped open again. I tried to get comfortable, squatting on the dusty floor of the cave. When I tried to adjust my position, I put my hand on a sharp rock.

"Ah, that hurt!" I protested. Ricardo barely noticed. "I'm so thirsty, aren't you?"

This sparked him. "I've got an idea. If you empty your bag, I can hold it out and try to fill it up with rainwater."

Bag? The sparkly party purse I still had with me from the barbecue was specially decorated for me by Katani! No way was I going to get it all wet. "No thanks, I can wait. But that was a good idea."

"It might not be raining later."

"Then we'll just leave, right?"

He was quiet for a moment. "Maybe they're out there, in the rain, searching for us," he said.

"Yeah, I'll bet they are. Or just waiting for the storm to pass to come get us. They'll be here soon. We'll be okay." I grabbed his hand and gave it a squeeze. He gave me a squeeze back. Maybe he was glad I was here too.

"We're not going to be too popular if they have to look for us in this storm."

I'm already expelled from the popularity contest, I figured.

I shifted on my spot a number of times. I couldn't just sit still. The nerve-shattering cracks of thunder and the blinding flashes of lightning came so regularly that I could predict them. I started to think about the thunder and lightning that would soon shoot out from my sister. Seriously, being stuck in a creepy cave was nothing compared to what Elena Maria might do to me when I got out of the cave. Having her beautiful party ruined because I caused a big commotion would upset her, and I wouldn't blame her one bit.

And that was *if* I ever saw my sister again. I shivered to think that the storm could continue for hours, possibly through to the morning and maybe all day. I decided that as soon as it got light, downpour or not, I would start walking back to the ranch.

"Aunt Lourdes is going to tell my mom to ground me for life when she hears about this."

"Will she really?"

"I don't think so, but Aunt Lourdes is really strict sometimes."

"Well, I bet she's nothing compared to my parents. They won't let me do anything!"

"Is that why you keep breaking all their rules?" I asked him. "Going in the living room, coming out to this cave . . ."

"Yeah, I guess so," he said. Then he thought a minute. "But I also just get so interested in things, you know? Like showing you the art. And hunting for 'dillos. And I sort of know in the back of my head that I shouldn't do it, but . . . then I get excited."

"Have you tried talking to your parents about it? I mean, maybe if they knew you just did that stuff because you were curious, not just to be bad—"

"No way," he interrupted me. "My parents think I'm like a baby. They would never understand."

We sat there in silence again for another few minutes.

"It's like this whole trip is going wrong for me," I said finally. "First you and I break the most beautiful piece of glass art I've ever seen. Then the police have to track me down at the River Walk, and now we're stuck in some crazy cave out in the middle of nowhere and it's dark and raining and creepy in here and . . . and . . . I just want to go home!" I felt tears coming and rested my head on my knees again with my arms wrapped around me like I was giving myself a big hug. I definitely needed one. But I didn't want Ricardo to know I was crying.

"It's okay, Isabel," he told me. "Don't freak out. It's not

so bad in here. I mean, at least we're dry. And my mom doesn't know it was us who broke the eagle, so that's okay too."

"Yeah, about that," I said, sniffling back my tears. "I don't think that's okay. Your mom is going to start asking questions, and if she accuses somebody like . . ."

"Maybe . . . Mercedes?" Ricardo offered.

Oh, no. "You really think so?" I felt faint. This was awful. Poor Mercedes.

"Well, probably," he reasoned. "She dusts in the living room every day, and hardly anybody else ever goes in there. Fonzie and Tony and me aren't allowed."

I gulped. "Do you think your mom would fire her?"

"She might."

"Ricardo! I can't believe how calm you're being. Do you know what this means? We can't let Mercedes lose her job because *we* broke something! We have to tell your Mom!"

"Isabel, *chica*, calm down," he said. "My mom hasn't said anything about firing anybody yet. Let's wait and see if she does it, okay? Maybe she'll just get over it."

"*Get over it?*" I couldn't believe he was being so dense. "She said that piece meant a lot to her, Rico. She sounded so sad that it was broken."

"She did?" Finally Ricardo sounded guilty.

"Yeah. She did."

We faced each other in the dark, not saying anything.

"I don't think saying nothing is right, Ricardo," I went on. "My friend Avery says that you have to step up to the plate and take the medicine when you've done something wrong. And I've been avoiding that all day today."

"Let's just wait and see what happens, Isabel," Ricardo repeated.

I gave up trying to convince him. Suddenly I was really tired, and having some big confession scene wasn't something I wanted to do anyway. And maybe he was right—maybe the whole thing would just go away. In the darkness I squeezed my eyes shut and crossed my fingers. *I wish everything would be okay. I wish everything would be okay. I wish everything would*—

Suddenly Ricardo got up. "My legs hurt." He flipped on the flashlight. "Let's go exploring."

I sprang up and dusted off the seat of my pants. "Are you crazy? What if we wake up a bear and it eats us? Of course, if that happens, we won't have to face your mom," I added sarcastically.

"There are no bears here. Only scorpions, tarantulas, and rattlesnakes."

I froze, but then ran after him so as not to be left in the dark. "You're kidding, right?" He didn't answer.

We moved slowly, close to the wall. In just a few feet the path narrowed and was impassable. He stooped to get past the low ceiling. I was still on the other side and was plunged immediately into darkness. The light reappeared when he pointed it at me. It disappeared again.

"Ricardo! Come back! Don't play games with me!"

"Oooh," he said, frightened or worried, I couldn't say. He rushed back to the crevice and stuck his head out. "You've got to get over here. It's like a little room in here."

"No! There might be spiders!"

"There's nothing in here. Come on, just do it." Once again he extended his hand, and I had no choice but to accept. I almost bumped my head on the way through, but on the other side I saw we had entered a big cavern. I couldn't hear the pounding rain anymore.

It was perfectly dry in here. It smelled strongly of dirt and old, cold air. The floor was sandy. Ricardo followed one wall with the light. It went on for yards, then seemed to form a corner. "Follow me," he said.

As we went deeper into the cave, I made a mental picture that if I stayed close to this wall, I could always find my way out if I just reversed my steps. Eventually we entered an even larger room, with taller walls and a ceiling that was too far overhead for the flashlight.

"Wow," Ricardo said. "I'll bet nobody even knows this place exists. We may be the first people to be here!"

I was speechless. The first people ever! This was better than a tea-party room for fairies. This was a chamber, a perfect hideaway. If we were closer to the ocean I would have said this was the ultimate pirate's lair. Ricardo walked a few yards to the middle of the room and dropped to his knees in the sand. "Hey, this ground is soft. We can camp out here till daybreak."

"No way!" The place was amazing, but it gave me a creepy feeling. "Let's get back to the other side. Maybe the rain's stopped by now."

"Fat chance, Isabel. Take it easy, will you? Nothing's going to happen to us here. Nobody even knows there's a cave here. And it's quiet. Maybe we can get some sleep." He took off his glasses and lay on his back.

"Who can sleep? We're lost in a cave!" I heard myself freak out.

"We're not lost. You've lost your mind, that's all. Just chill for a minute."

I knew he was right. I needed to calm down, but something about this space scared me. I wanted to go back to the cave entrance.

Instead, I flopped down on the soft ground and stared into the darkness, feeling kind of hopeless. I wanted to write a letter of apology to my parents, my sister and her friends, and to Ricardo's parents, who'd done so much for our family this week. I could just imagine them all wandering around out there in the rain, searching for us. My mom would be so worried—out of her mind by now, probably. And, of course, I wanted to apologize for breaking that beautiful eagle.

I pulled a little pad of paper out of my purse. Ricardo must have heard the paper rustling, because he asked, "Are you making a map of the place?"

I didn't answer.

"Here, use this." Ricardo tossed me the flashlight.

It helped. I felt so much better just holding the light in my lap. "I'm just writing a few notes to myself about . . . tonight."

"Are you a writer? Is that why you carry a notebook?"

"No, not a writer." I paused. Should I go on? "I do draw, though. I'm the staff cartoonist for our school newspaper."

"You are? What a great job! Do you draw funny cartoons or political cartoons?"

How to answer this one? "I, uh, I've tried a little of both. But mostly I just focus on things that are important to me. I like to draw birds the most."

"Isabel, you're so sharp. I'll bet you've come up with some pretty hot cartoons."

Me? Sharp? I smiled, thankful that he could not see me. "Actually, I like to think that my cartoons are positive and help people see human silliness . . . and stuff."

"So is that what you want to do when you grow up?"

"I don't know. I'd like to be an artist when I'm older. But I know it's hard to make a living on art."

"You could become a sketch artist in a courtroom." I'd never thought about that. "Or a fashion designer. You need to know how to draw to do that, right?"

"Yep. My friend Katani wants to be a fashion designer. And the CEO of her own company. I like computer animation a lot. I think that would be lots of fun. But right now, I'm concentrating on line drawing. Single-panel cartoons with one-sentence captions that get right to the point."

I spent a few minutes arranging the flashlight on my lap so that I could hold the pad steady with one hand and write with the other. I was trying to draw an armadillo. I looked at the sand in front of me, wondering how I should start, when I noticed something that looked out of place in the sand, a faint criss-cross pattern. It didn't move, so I figured there was nothing alive under there.

I touched it. Definitely harmless. I brushed off the dirt and lifted up something stiff. "Hey, look," I said. "Somebody's wallet."

"Is there money in it?"

"I don't think so. It looks like a bag." I aimed the flashlight. The bag was made of leather or string, a crudely worked piece that was stiff as a board. I dangled it by a string at one end.

Ricardo's eyes were big as quarters. He took it from me and examined it. I directed the light low, so it didn't get in his eyes.

I watched him as he held the bag in front of his eyes. He ran his finger over the woven strips, tried to bend it into a bag shape. He poked a finger through a hole at the bottom. I heard his breath quicken.

I saw the look on his face change with excitement. As I watched him, he mumbled, "Wow wow wow." I noticed something else: a big, black shadow on the wall behind him. My heart nearly stopped as my hand automatically drew the flashlight up the wall. This thing went way up, and as it did, strange lines protruded from the sides.

"Ricardo—"

"Put the light on this, Izzy. I think we've stumbled onto something big."

"No," I said calmly. "Something bigger." I aimed the flashlight up. The giant, black rectangle was crowned with a lopsided circle. More crazy lines, like skinny lightning bolts, protruded from the circle.

Both of us gasped simultaneously. Before us was a painting on the cave wall: enormous, eerie, and incredible. I swept the walls to either side of the image and saw smaller figures that looked like people and animals.

We faced each other, and screamed at the same time: *"Oh my gosh!"* and *"¡Dios mío!"* Our voices echoed off the walls.

"Gimme that," he said, taking the light from me. He swung it wildly, yelling delightedly as he continued to spotlight more figures.

I dropped to the floor and ran my fingers through the sand. I dug up other items: sticks, rocks, and several funny things that I didn't recognize at first: short stubs of wood with bristly fibers tied in a bunch at one end. Brushes! I scrambled my hands in the sand wildly, then stopped abruptly. If this was what I thought it was, then it was best to step . . . back . . . quickly.

I stood, and tiptoed gingerly away. This was a sacred space. I could feel it. We should not disturb an inch of it.

Ricardo whooped, creating an echo in the chamber that sounded perfectly musical. "Isabel! Do you realize what this is?"

"Don't touch anything! Stop!" He almost fell over from my urgent command. "I think this bag belonged to somebody. From a long time ago."

"I've seen pictures of stuff like this at museums. These could be thousands of years old!" he exclaimed.

I lost my balance. I felt faint.

"Maybe not that old," I said. "Look at what else there is. I think these things fell out of the pouch." I pointed to items in the sand. We dropped to our knees and hunched over as far as we could to examine them without touching them.

He pointed at one of the rocks with a jagged edge. "That's a tool, for sure. I'd stake my life on it. What are those?" He pointed at the wooden stubs.

"I think they might be paintbrushes."

He shined the light on one. A dark red color was definitely visible on the fibers. "You're right! This has to be what they used," he said. "There's a bunch of red figures over at that end." We both looked at the stash as if we'd found a pot of gold.

"We can't touch anything," I reminded him. "But help me out. Shine the light on some of these pictures so I can draw them."

"Pictographs. They're called pictographs. I read all about them in my history class at school." I looked into Ricardo's eyes. He was as excited as I was.

We got to work immediately. My hands trembled. I started to laugh.

"I'm so nervous, I can barely hold the pen!"

"Take your time. We're not going anywhere. Isabel, you're going to be famous."

"No way," I said. "I'm only a school newspaper cartoonist, remember?"

"You've made a major discovery here. I'm sure of it."

"You mean *we* made a discovery."

"No," he said. "You saw the pouch. You saw the pictures."

"And you brought me in here."

I tried to draw as fast as I could. Ricardo said he counted twenty-six images, but wasn't sure he caught them all. As I sketched on the little pad of paper, we discussed what we thought the pictographs represented. Some of the pictures were obvious: the sun, a deer, a rabbit with really long ears, and other stuff. He said dogs, I said coyotes. The human figures stumped us, though. They were definitely weird.

"I think they're shamans," he said. "I remember pictures like this from my history book. The squiggly lines coming out of their heads means they're in a trance. This place *is* called *Los Mitotes*."

Los mitotes. The dances. Did ancient shamans have wild dances in this cave thousands of years ago? A little shiver went down my spine as I flashed the light on the drawings again. Right then, it seemed like anything was possible.

CHAPTER

10

Swing Yer Partner

The excitement over our discovery was making me shake inside. I don't know how long it took me to sketch the drawings, but I felt Ricardo and I did a good job documenting the find without disturbing it. Although I had Elena Maria's camera with me, I took only three photographs. I remembered from our class trip to Boston's Museum of Fine Arts that using the flash might harm the ancient artwork, but I had no choice. We needed something better than my drawings to explain this. I split the wall art into two photos, and took a close-up shot of the items in the sand. Here I was, shooting prehistoric pictures drawn by ancient people. Again, my fingers began to tingle.

Eventually, though, I was tired and thirsty. A strange energy buzzed through me. Ricardo and I worked well together. He had some decent guesses when I couldn't figure out an image. When we were done, we squeezed slowly back through the tiny crevice and plopped ourselves in the exact same spots as before, near the entrance to the cave. I couldn't take it anymore.

"Here," I said, dumping the stuff out of my purse and shoving it at him. *Sorry, Katani,* I apologized silently.

Without a second thought he pushed the purse in on the sides to square it up, then extended his arm outside as far as he could, soaking his sleeve beyond his shoulder. "Brrr! Cold!"

But he continued to hold out his arm until the purse filled with rainwater. I watched in amazement. "Drink, drink fast," he said when he retracted it. "It's not watertight." Ricardo was turning out to be the kind of person that you would want with you during a disaster.

I rapidly gulped a couple of swigs and passed it back to him. He filled it again and drank, then filled it and passed it to me. We went through several rounds before he complained about his wet sleeve again.

"Thank you. That really was a great idea," I admitted.

With my belly full of water, I started to relax. We tried to estimate about how long we'd been trapped in the cave. It was hopeless. It could have been four hours or six, or more. The rain fell steadily, but the thunder and lightning eventually faded. I soon forgot about the pictographs and my family and fell asleep.

I felt my ankle shake. Ricardo was nudging me. I rose and pushed the hair out of my face.

Ricardo shone the flashlight at something outside. "Come look at this."

The fog of sleep would not lift. I blinked. I knew where

I was, but something had changed. The rain sounded a little lighter, but it wasn't over. Outside it was still pitch-black.

"Hurry up!" he whispered.

I weighed two hundred pounds with sleep, but I crawled over to him anyway. I squinted in the light and saw two ugly forms. A couple of armadillos rooted at the base of a shrub, shielded from the rain by the foliage.

"Mission accomplished," Ricardo said.

"Assignment complete," I agreed.

We high-fived and watched them some more.

"They're so ugly, but cute!" I breathed. "Almost like baby dinosaurs." I couldn't wait to tell Avery. She would want to hear every little detail. Animals were one of her main passions in life.

"Yeah, everybody thinks they're so cute. But look at those freaky things."

One of the animals stopped, alerted by our voices. Compared to its torso, the head was small. It had adorable ears. But the body was something else. It looked positively prehistoric. Its skin looked hard, like that of a crocodile or an elephant—or even a rhinoceros—and its middle was segmented in bands. Its long, thin tail also had defined segments, which I found particularly gross. It reminded me of a *tlacuache,* or possum.

"Ew, it's got a *tlacuache* tail," I sneered. "Once when I was a little girl I saw a long, skinny, *naked* possum tail hanging out of a trash can. Ewwww!"

"Aw, *tlacuaches* are cute," Ricardo said.

"Not to me."

"Shhh!"

The 'dillos made gentle snorting sounds as they rooted for something to eat. One came closer to us. Sparse, wiry hairs stuck out of its skin. They glittered in the light. Armadillos were pretty cool. But I needed to rest. Too much had happened.

I went back to the wall and curled up. Ricardo observed a little longer, then turned out the flashlight. The rain was softer now. I heard the animals snuffling.

"Rico?"

A pause, and then: "What?"

"Is *tlacuache* a Spanish word? Or is it na . . . na—"

"Nahuatl, Isabel. Na-wah-tuuuullllll." He fell asleep even faster than me.

Rescue Squad

The sound of birds singing a pretty song woke me. The instant I scrambled, Ricardo was up.

"They're here," he said.

"Who?"

"Can't you hear them?" He reached for a shoe that had somehow fallen off during the night.

I grabbed my stuff and followed him out. The sun peeked through the puffy clouds and everything smelled clean and new. It felt glorious. We had survived.

Ricardo reached the ledge where he'd tied Rasquatch to the tree. He waited for me to catch up. "Well, here goes," he said, and ran down the path to the base of the hill.

"The 'dillos made gentle snorting sounds as they rooted for something to eat. One came closer to us."

He waved his arms at a faraway bouncing pickup truck. It sped in our direction.

As it got closer we whooped and hollered, thrilled to be rescued. The truck didn't slow down until it was practically on top of us. Uncle Hector rushed out of the cab. We clammed up quickly. He looked very sad. Or was he really angry?

"Children," he said calmly. "What happened?"

"Oh, I'm sorry, Dad. Really I am."

"Whaaat happened, Ricardo?" he demanded.

Neither of us knew where to start.

Enrique slowly emerged from the pickup, looking at us as if he was seeing ghosts. Uncle Hector nodded to him, indicating that all was okay.

"Enrique found the horse this morning. Saddled with your *bolsa*, son. Rasquatch was grazing out in the open, by the patio." He made a sound like he was fighting back tears. "We didn't know what to think!"

Enrique stood by my uncle. The two looked very relieved. Uncle Hector continued. "We checked your room, Ricardo. You weren't there. The two of us just got in the truck and started looking for you."

We both stared down at our shoes.

"Isabel, I had no idea you'd be out here, too. Are you okay, *mamacita*?"

"Yes, Tío. It was the most amazing thing. We—"

Ricardo kicked me. We walked to the truck. Ricardo and I climbed into the rear of the cab, and we drove away. Nobody spoke until Ricardo asked, "When did you start looking for us, Dad?"

"Not even a half hour ago. As soon as Enrique found the horse. How long have you been out here?"

Ricardo squinched his eyes, not eager to reveal the truth. "Since last night."

Uncle Hector slammed on the brakes. He shifted his body to face us. "Last night?" My uncle's jaw dropped. "What? Where? How?"

"We left on Rasquatch after dinner. We were looking for armadillos, but the horse got spooked by the thunder. We hid in a cave to stay dry."

Enrique gasped. Uncle Hector's eyebrows shot up.

"A cave?"

We nodded.

He slowly turned around and looked out the windshield. "Son, you're going to have to explain every single detail when we get home . . . to me. I don't intend to tell your mothers about this. Those sweet ladies have enough to worry about today."

Ricardo and I looked at each other. No one even knew we were gone. Nobody missed us.

We pulled into the carport. Uncle Hector looked at me strangely as he reminded me about rehearsal for the big *quinceañera* waltz later that morning. I apologized to my uncle for making him worry and hurried away. I wanted to be a hundred miles away from Ricardo's discussion with his father.

I heard Freckles the rooster crow as if he were welcoming me home. I reached the patio and smacked right into Elena Maria. "Enrique just told me about the horse and Ricardo. Fidencia and I checked your room to see if you knew what happened to him this morning, and you were gone! Your bed wasn't even slept in! Isabel, what is going on here?" My sister was clearly bewildered. All that time in the cave I was afraid that everyone was sick with worry about me—and nobody even noticed I was gone!

"Never mind! I'll fill you in later. I need some sleep." I started to my room.

"Isabel." Elena Maria stepped in front of me and blocked my way. "You don't get it. Uncle Hector and Enrique and Fidencia and I just had the scare of a lifetime, and you're *walking away*? With no explanation? Why are you acting this way?" She shook my arm.

"What way?"

"Like this! Like an attention hog. Like a princess. You just have to have the spotlight, don't you?"

"Me? I'm not acting like a princess . . . oh, never mind." Couldn't she see that she was the one acting like a princess? I squeezed past her.

"Isabel!" she cried. "Even if you don't care about what's going on with me, maybe at least you'll care about what's going on with Dad!"

I stopped and turned around. "What?"

She looked close to tears. "He called late last night. His flight was cancelled because of the storm, and he's stuck in Tulsa. He's trying to figure out whether he can get here in time."

Dad wasn't going to be there for the *quince*? I almost

felt like crying too. "I'm sure he'll make it, Elena Maria," I managed to choke out.

"What if he doesn't?" she replied sadly.

"Elena Maria, Papa will be here. I know he will." She nodded, and for a moment I thought she was going to hug me. But she didn't. She just shrugged and walked away.

I turned and ran into the house, wanting to be anywhere but near my sister. I didn't want to cry and get her more upset. My father not coming—how could that be?

Fidencia intercepted me in the kitchen. "Praise heaven and earth that my little one is alive and safe!" she cried in Spanish, taking my face in her hands. She fed me breakfast and I scarfed it up, even though I was sad. I started with fluffy scrambled eggs with Mexican sausage and sides of refried beans and French-fried potato cubes. The salsa I dumped on my eggs was astonishingly delicious, with hot-off-the-skillet flour tortillas drenched in butter. *At least I'm welcome in the kitchen,* I thought.

I was feeling pretty sorry for myself when I finally flopped onto my bed. I couldn't believe I was so unimportant to my sister's *quinceañera* that nobody even missed me at the barbecue. And Dad maybe not coming—that was the worst news I'd heard this whole trip. I pulled the covers over my head to block out the sunlight, and drifted off to sleep with visions of cave dwellers drifting through my brain.

Cave Morning

Aunt Inez and Uncle Hector's house had the perfect layout for a party, with a beautiful patio and a giant family room that was as big as a ballroom. That's where everyone assembled late in the morning to learn the traditional couples' waltz that the honor court always performs at a *quinceañera*. Tony and Fonzie introduced more relatives from my mother's side of the family to fill out Elena Maria's honor court: Samuel and Gilberto, and Sonia, Alisa, and Delia. Irma stood off to the side with Elena Maria. She seemed to be consoling her. Ricardo stationed himself by the CD player, sorting a stack of CDs.

On the other side of the room, I noticed my mom walk in quietly and take a seat in a big, comfy chair by a huge window. I'd never been so happy to see my mom in my whole life! After our night in the cave, I needed a hug.

I dashed over to her. "Mamiiii!" I cried, throwing myself into the giant chair next to her and giving her a hug all at the same time. She smiled in surprise and hugged me back.

"Hello, *mi 'jita*," she said, stroking my hair and sounding confused but pleased. "Why do I deserve such a nice greeting?"

I really wanted to tell her about my scary night in the cave, but like Uncle Hector said, I didn't want to upset her. "No reason," I said finally.

Fortunately, she didn't have time to ask me any more questions, because Uncle Hector dashed in, clapping his hands. "Okay! Gather round, please."

We all formed a circle around him. He nodded at Ricardo, who pushed a button on the CD player. A beautiful, slowish, sort of classical-sounding song began. Uncle

Hector gently bobbed his head in time to the music then signaled Ricardo: Cut!

"That, young friends, is a traditional waltz, one performed more often at weddings than at *quinces*, but we figured it could work. After all, your parents"—he looked at his three sons—"and your parents"—he looked from Elena Maria to me—"danced to this tune at their own weddings. And since we're celebrating the *quinceañera* of my dear niece, well, you can understand why we chose it." He gave my mother a million-dollar grin.

Was Mom part of the "we" who picked that song? I wondered. From her reaction—a tight-lipped smile and a polite nod—it didn't look like it. No big mystery there: Everything about the *quinceañera* seemed to be decided by Uncle Hector and Aunt Inez, the producer/director/set decorators for this whole production.

"Antonio," my uncle called, then spoke to the group. "Allow us to demonstrate."

"Aw, Pop!"

"*Ándale, ándale,*" he said, beckoning Tony with his hand. "This is no time for shyness, son."

They both assumed the lead dancer's position, holding up their right arms. Uncle Hector tried to raise Tony's left hand, but Tony wouldn't budge. Tony countered by putting his hand on his father's waist, which confused my uncle even more. It was too funny. Andy and Scott jumped up and started dancing a polka. I almost fell over laughing. Even Elena Maria was laughing her head off. It felt great to see my sister back to her upbeat, friendly self.

"Get serious, please. Stand there and let me be the leader, Antonio." He took a few steps. Tony pouted but followed. "Scott, are you watching? This is how you will lead Elena Maria. Step, two, three. Step, two, three. And when the music changes, stop, hold her hand high, and let her twiiiirl like a ballerina." Tony rotated awkwardly and I stifled a giggle. "Yes, like that! And then it's back to step, two, three, step, two, three." He gave the signal to Ricardo to stop the music. "And there you have it. Think you can do it?"

Tony bowed. Everybody clapped.

"Wonderful. Everybody find your partner and let's give it a try. I'll count out loud so we can keep time." He took Ricardo's place at the CD player so that Ricardo could join me. "And a-one, and a-two, and a—"

The music began. Everybody started step-two-three-ing and bumped into one another. None of the girls twirled in the proper direction. The boys awkwardly stuck their arms out when the girls spun. Of course I was paired with Ricardo. We were both so exhausted that we could barely move our feet, much less keep time with music.

Soon the dance was total chaos. Uncle Hector stopped the music.

"Ahem. Let's try it again. Form a circle. You," he said to Andy, "stand there. Delia, get closer. Tony, Irma, stand in the center and show everyone what to do."

He started the music again, and instructed loudly, "Step, two, three, step, two, three, step, two, three, twiiirl!"

Ricardo was a terrible dancer to follow. His glasses

kept slipping off his nose, and when he stopped to fix them our timing went off even more. It was a bad scene. If our performance hadn't been so funny, it would have been on my list of most embarrassing moments.

"How'd it go with your father this morning?" I whispered between giggles.

"Oh, man! He was upset, but he was grateful I wasn't hurt. He said he would decide on what my 'consequences' would be later. I'll probably just have to do more chores and stuff. No big deal."

I felt terrible. Why should Ricardo have to do chores, but not me? "What did he say about the cave paintings?"

"I didn't tell him! I don't think he even really knows what happened to us. He was just relieved that my mother didn't know. I think we're home free."

"How long can we keep the truth from our moms? They're bound to figure out soon that we spent the night in the cave. My sister might even tell. I'm sure Enrique told Fidencia, and if I know my sister, she probably got Fidencia to tell her."

He glanced around nervously. "Not if we can help it."

"But the cave art—"

"We can bring it up after the party. Everybody will be all chilled out. We don't want to upset your sister's party any more."

I agreed and looked around for my mom, but her chair was empty. She was gone. That was weird. Why would she walk out in the middle of the rehearsal? I thought I knew— my aunt and uncle were taking over all the party planning, and leaving her with nothing to do. But would my mom really get jealous like that? That wasn't her style.

Ricardo and I kept on waltzing but after a few rounds we got dizzy. We were both so tired it was getting hard to stand up. After a while we just plodded in a circle. The "twirl" became a chance to drop my arms and rotate absentmindedly. I tripped over my own feet.

"Isabel, stay sharp," my uncle shouted. "Ricardo, grab her by the waist. Don't be afraid of her, son."

Ricardo's brothers hooted. I felt my cheeks burn, and Ricardo turned as red as a cherry. Why did adults always have to be so embarrassing? To distract myself from our humiliation, I checked out everybody else. Only Irma and Tony seemed to know what they were doing. The worst was Scott. With the ankle support still strapped to his foot, he could not step-two-three smoothly enough. Elena Maria kept tripping over his foot. Soon she was sprawled on the floor.

"Pardon me!" Scott said. He imitated a gentleman's moves and put a hand on his stomach. He bent over and held out his other hand to help her up. Elena Maria did not think he was funny at all. In fact, she looked like she'd had about enough.

"*Ayeeeeeee!*" She ran screaming from the room. You could tell Scott felt really bad. He looked totally crushed.

"Oh, she's hurt! Should I follow her?" He took off, stomping like a peg-legged pirate.

I blocked him. "Scott, you stay here and practice"— I looked around—"with Ricardo. I'll help my sister."

I slipped out of the room before Uncle Hector could stop me.

I searched the house but couldn't find her. She wasn't in her bedroom, the living room, or the kitchen, where I almost stepped on Freckles, who squawked and flew up near my face, nearly giving me a heart attack. Finally I heard her, sobbing quietly from behind a bathroom door. I waited a moment before I knocked.

"Who is it?" she asked, her voice thick with tears.

"It's only me. Can I come in?"

"Go away. I'm not in the mood."

I took a deep breath. "Elena, please let me come in."

She unlocked the door and opened it a crack. I squeezed through the narrow opening. The tiny bathroom was barely big enough for both of us. She stood with her back to me, and I heard her choke back tears.

I very carefully put my hand on her shoulder and said, "Elena, I know you're superstressed. And I'm really sorry if I made you even more stressed than you already were. I'm sorry I've been such a pest."

She whirled around. I instinctively hugged her. She cried into my shoulder. I felt so sad, but grateful to be hugging my sister again.

"Izzy, it's not just you. It's Papa. Where is he? He was going to teach us the waltz. Not Uncle Hector, who's kind of klutzy if you ask me. And Papa's supposed to be my partner for the first dance. This is turning out all wrong."

This was an important moment, so I chose my words carefully. "No, it's not wrong. It's just not turning out the way you imagined it. You had all these dreams, and nothing is the way you thought it would be. But Mom promised that Dad is coming . . . and all your friends are having an incredible time. A week on a ranch in Texas is very cool. You'll see, they'll be talking about your party for weeks."

She snuffled and gave me a kiss. Her tears were ending. "Scott is a terrible dancer! How was I supposed to know?" She noticed herself in the mirror. "Eek! I look like I'm melting! Now what do I do? Everyone's going to know I was crying." She tried really hard to hold back some big tears.

I stroked her hair. "I know what you mean about Scott. I don't get it. He's so athletic. Maybe he's just nervous because he likes you so much."

"Do you think so?" she asked, dabbing at her eye.

"Yes, I think that's it. Look, why don't you take a break? I'll tell everybody the rehearsal is off for now. If the boss needs a break, then everybody gets a break too."

"Me, the boss." Her mood lightened. "You're so funny, Izzy. The only boss around here is . . ." She looked around suspiciously.

"Tía Inez," we said together. We cracked up and hugged. My sister was back!

Part Two
Dance Fever

CHAPTER

11

Waltz Recycled

I marched back to the rehearsal room, ready to make up for all my mishaps of the past few days. "Everyone, my sister's not feeling so hot right now," I announced. "She's totally stressed about this whole party and whether my dad's going to make it. So, she asked me to tell you rehearsal is postponed until later today."

The honor court reacted slowly to the unexpected change of plans. Alisa and Sonia suggested swimming. The boys decided to visit the calf pens, where Tony promised to show them some rope tricks. Soon the only ones left in the room were Ricardo and me. Finally. This was the perfect opportunity to get in touch with the BSG!

"*Amigo*," I said, "I need some technical assistance. Show me the way to the computer."

He led me to his father's office. Sitting on the desk was my dream computer. I'm into computer animation as well as hand-drawn cartoons, so I know a little about computers, and this one had the works: a huge, flat, wide-screen monitor with a built-in webcam and a very cool-looking silver keyboard. I could hardly wait to get my hands on it.

"You're so lucky!" I breathed, sitting down at the huge desk. I felt like Alice in Wonderland after she drank the shrinking potion—my feet didn't even come close to touching the floor!

"I guess," Ricardo said, shrugging, as I clicked on the browser icon. The little hourglass appeared on the screen, and we waited . . . and waited. Finally a blank Web page showed up with the message: "Connection timed out."

"Okay, what now?" I asked. Ricardo stared at the screen, waiting for something to happen. Nothing happened.

"Is your system slow, or is there a problem?" I asked. "Should I restart it or something?"

"What do you need the computer for, anyway?"

More frustration. "My sister is starting to go nuts because my father can't tell us exactly when he's coming. I want to e-mail him. I think he can read it on his cell phone." Almost as important, however, was the BSG. "And my friends, too. I promised I'd keep in touch and tell them about life on the ranch. I'm also dying to see if any of them have sent me anything."

"Hold on," Ricardo said. He clicked on the icon again, then leaned forward on the desk, resting his head on both hands just inches from the giant screen.

And I held on. I waited again. I leaned back in the giant

chair and swung my legs. I eyeballed the room repeatedly, noticing a huge landscape in a big, gold frame hanging on the wall opposite me. Was that a Diego Rivera too? Even in an office this family had priceless art!

Ricardo continued to stare at the "Connection timed out" message.

"You know, you really are lucky to have all of this," I told him again, while we waited.

He hunched up his shoulders. "All of what?" he mumbled.

Um, hello. "All of *this*," I said. "The amazing art collection. A ranch with an amazing cave. This incredible house!" I jumped up and stood in the middle of the room, throwing out my arms. "Not to mention this fabulous computer, which doesn't seem to want to connect."

But Ricardo just hunched up even more and wouldn't look at me. "Yeah, I'm a lucky guy," he said a little sarcastically.

I didn't understand my cousin. It was like sometimes he loved to show off all the great stuff his family had, but then other times he wanted to act like it didn't exist.

"Hey," I shook his shoulder. "I want to talk to my friends."

"Hold on, Izzy," he said. "We don't have the best connection out here sometimes."

"Sometimes? Like, how much of the time?"

"Like . . . you know, sometimes."

"Should we restart it?" I asked. My frustration was mounting.

"Uhh, it's my dad's computer. . . . He told me not to mess with it."

Here we go again. Ricardo was messing with something he wasn't supposed to mess with. "Don't you have computer of your own?" I asked impatiently. "Elena Maria and I share one at home."

"My parents say I'm not old enough," he grumbled.

"I can try again later," I said quickly. I felt bad that my cousin was being treated like a baby, so I changed the subject. "I just can't understand why it's taking so long for my father to get here," I whined. "Aren't you so tired, Rico? Last night was too *crazy!* And I'm dying to tell somebody about our discovery."

"Me too. Isabel, this could be something big . . . really big." His eyes actually glowed as he talked. "But we really should wait until after the *quinceañera*. Your family will still be here. Everyone should be more relaxed by then, and Elena will be chilled out after she has her star moment."

"You know, you're right, Rico." I stared up at a painting of a dancer. "We have to chill. This party is getting intense. But I think I can help get this waltz on the road. Go tell everyone to regroup in an hour. I've got a great idea."

Rocking the Waltz

I practically skipped back to the rehearsal room. The boys were sliding around in their socks. I noticed that Scott had finally removed the ankle brace. Excellent sign!

I clapped my hands and took charge. The success

of Elena Maria's most important birthday party ever depended on me. I decided to channel my Aunt Lourdes. "Listen up, people. We've got a program to put on. And my sister is going to be very unhappy if you guys don't *get the dance right*."

The boys exchanged uncomfortable glances. Most of the girls nodded, but I noticed that Jill was standing with her arms crossed and her head tilted to one side, looking skeptical.

"So I am going to give you a quick lesson in how to master a new dance in record-breaking time. First, we need—"

"*You're going to teach us* a dance?" Jill sneered. "Um, sorry, Isabel, but we really don't have time to play with you right now. We have to do a real dance at the *quince* tomorrow, and I think we should work on that. Not something a twelve-year-old just made up." She looked around to see who was with her. "Right, guys?"

Lauren looked at the ground. All the boys looked at one another uncomfortably. Not even one of my cousins spoke up for me! I could feel my face turning red. Maybe I couldn't help Elena Maria. Maybe this was all a big mistake.

"Actually . . . ," Scott started. Jill glared at him, but he went on. "Actually, I think Avery told me that Isabel was a dancer. And I even saw her dance in this talent show at their school one time."

I smiled. No wonder Elena had such a huge crush on Scott. He was one solid guy.

"Welllll . . . I used to be really into dancing," I told everybody. "I took a lot of classes for years. Mostly ballet, but other styles too, like jazz and hip-hop. But then I hurt my knee so I had to stop doing it. Now I just dance for fun, whenever I feel like it." I held my head high and looked at Jill. "Like now. So if anybody wants me to teach them a dance we can do for the waltz that I know my sister is absolutely going to love, we have to practice—now." I turned around, crossed my fingers, and hoped my dance troupe would follow my lead.

To my amazement, everybody started taking their places with their partners. I couldn't believe my speech had really worked! Jill was kind of still sneering a little as she took Alfonso's hand, but at least she didn't say anything else.

"Scott, I noticed you were playing indoor hockey without your foam brace. Does this mean your ankle's better?" I asked.

"Could be, Isabel. I just took it off a while ago to see how I can hold up. And look, I can skate!" He pushed off on one socked foot, sliding toward me.

"Good work, Michelle Kwan. Now everybody pay attention. I think it's time to give this waltz a hip-hop spin."

Fonzie snickered. "Hip-hop waltz? No such animal."

"What I mean, Alfonso, is that you take an old dance"—I started with a heel-toe—"and give it a cool makeover," I finished as I spun around and snapped.

My cousin Irma fell in step with me. In a matter of

minutes we choreographed a series of moves that cul-
minated in the spin: We froze. She krumped, I popped.
We both hit a dime stop, then started again. The crowd
whooped.

"Nice moves, Iz, Irma," Tony said. "Like a Texas two-
step, but with a lot of style. Hip and elegant."

"It's Isabel's Texas two-step," Scott declared.

The boys formed a line and started to work the beat.
The girls stood to the side and shadowed the boys' steps.
Delia and Alisa assumed a couple's position and improved
the spin routine that Irma and I had performed. Things
started to heat up.

Everybody practiced, then assembled as a group. It
happened so naturally. The boys nailed their moves and
helped the girls fall into rhythm with them. Ricardo and
I had it down in minutes. Piece of cake! I wanted to try it
with the music.

Just then Uncle Hector walked in, surprised by all the
activity. I signaled him to shush. Ricardo stood at the ready
by the CD player.

"Maestro." I motioned to Ricardo. The music started.

The column of dancers started the procession with a
glide. Every fourth step the boys made an intricate heel-toe
move and the girls followed with their own cool shimmy.
When it came time for the spin, the boys popped their
arms over the girls' heads while the girls circled delicately
beneath them.

I made the "cut" signal to Ricardo. The honor court
cheered. Uncle Hector clapped wildly.

"*¡Muy buen hecho!*" he said. "I like it! It has an old-world feel with a modern touch. How did you come up with this so quickly? Three hours ago you were all falling over your own feet!"

"It was Isabel," Scott informed him. I suddenly felt shy and looked down at my feet. "She totally whipped us into shape!"

"*Muchas gracias*, Isabel," Uncle Hector said to me, giving a slight bow. "Your sister will be thrilled. She is so lucky to have an *hermanita* like you to help out at her *quince*."

Now I was beaming from ear to ear. At last I had gotten something right!

The Romance of a Lifetime

That night, after dinner, Mom let me help her with the paper decorations again. She pulled out stacks of paper and cutting tools. She showed me how to fold the thin, colorful tissue and how to cut it with a pair of tiny, sharp scissors and a special knife. My breath caught when I opened up the folded square. I'd made random cuts, but when I laid it out the effect was dazzling.

Then I watched her lay a pattern on top of a stack of tissue paper and use a small chisel and hammer to cut through the whole stack at once. "After we finish, we can ask Mercedes to iron out the creases. The last step is to string them together and, presto, we have another banner of *papel picado*."

We worked in silence for a while, then I asked, "Mom, tell me again how you met Dad." I'd heard it so many times before, but I wanted to hear it again.

She looked down at me and smiled. "You like that story, don't you? Well, I met Jorge Maximiliano Martinez, your father, three years to the day before we married. We were both in our second year at university, and we met at a big local dance. My friend Nina kept talking about some boy she was supposed to meet there, but as soon as we arrived, she took off to dance with the first person who asked her.

"So I was left alone. I went to get some punch, and that's when I first saw him, but only from the back. He was helping a little old lady with her drink, and it was obvious she was very flattered by your father's attention to her. Your dad, he knew it too. I couldn't hear them, but I could tell by her face that he had her completely bewitched.

"My first thought was, 'What an egotistical guy.' So I leaned in to listen to them, and noticed that he smelled *terrific*. This got me interested. He was going on and on that the girl he was supposed to meet was dancing with somebody else, and so he asked the *viejita* if she would dance with him. It was funny to see, Isabel. The little old lady did not want to dance at all. She kept reassuring him that there were plenty of young ladies for him to choose from, and that's when I knew it was time to act.

"I just put myself right between them and coolly asked, 'Do I hear a request for a dance partner?' and that was it. He took one look at me and I saw it in his face: He was hit with the lightning bolt of love. Which made me feel like the queen of the universe, by the way. And he was just so handsome, I wanted to melt."

I loved looking at my mom's face when she got to this point of the story. She was looking off into the distance, smiling. "He was just about to ask me to dance, too, when who shows up? Nina! Oof, I wanted to strangle her for her bad timing. When he saw her, of course he asked her to dance instead. It was only proper—after all, she was supposed to be his date. Even after he asked her she acted all offended, accusing him of not looking for her when he got there. But I knew the truth. Nina just wanted to cover up for the fact that *she* hadn't looked for *him*! So I spoke up. 'Is this the boy you said you were going to meet here?'

"He said, 'You two know each other?' I ignored his question and said to Nina, 'Why, he's been here at the punch bowl since we walked in. You're the one who went straight to the dance floor as soon as we got here.' Another song was starting, and sure enough, who walks up right behind her but another boy—saying she had already promised to dance this one with him!

"That left just me and your father. He took my hand, led me to the dance floor, and by the time Nina was able to get away from that other boy, well . . . we were already dancing, and dancing, and dancing. And before we knew it, the evening was over. Nina had already left, he walked me home, and I know as sure as the sun rises that he would have asked me to marry him that night, except your father wanted to do the right thing and *court me*. And so he did. For two years! We got married on the third anniversary of our first dance."

"But how did you know he was the right one, Mom?"

She shrugged her shoulders and shook her head. "Hard to say. It's just a feeling. And also, we just had so much in common."

"What did you have in common?" I knew the answers to these questions, but I asked anyway, just to keep her talking. She was right—I loved to hear this story!

"Why, accounting, of course. He loved the world of numbers as much as I did. Isabel, I right away saw his kindness, his reliability. He was a man I could depend on. And after I met his parents, that did it. I loved his family! Margarito and Maria, what a pair."

I sighed. "Did you hear from Papa? Did he get another flight yet?"

She looked quickly down at the piece of paper in her hands. Was that a little trace of a smile I could see? "I would not worry about him too much, *mi amor*," she told me. "Your father will move mountains to get here."

"Mom, you look like a bird who just swallowed a cat," I joked. "Do you know something you're not telling us?"

"Mmmm . . . it seems that the air here in Texas is full of secrets, wouldn't you say?" she answered mysteriously before going back to her work.

She was right about that one. More secrets than I ever wanted to know!

12

"Witte" Way Did He Go?

I opened the shutters to find another *magnífico* Texas Hill Country scene. The sun was far above the horizon, and the silver clouds looked picture-perfect. The singing birds turned out to be robins, hundreds of them, roosting on branches, pecking at the ground, singing their little hearts out. Bluebonnets were starting to sprout. Springtime in Texas!

How could anyone not be happy on a day like this? I sighed as I pushed away the vision of a glass tip flying through the air. I slipped into my favorite jeans, the ones with the patch of a baby penguin sewn on the back pocket, and at record speed laced up my sneakers and threw on a cool purple T-shirt that Katani loaned me before I left. I was all ready to meet this totally kickin' day.

The kitchen was a beehive of girl activity when I arrived. Elena & Co., Mom, and Aunt Inez were all ready to go shopping—shoe shopping—at the River Walk again. After my last shopping disaster with the *quince* posse I was ready to take a pass, when a fat little robin perched on the window. It practically chirped, *Go to the Blue Turtle Gallery, and tell Xochitl and her dad about the cave drawings.*

"Can I go with you? I want to visit Xochitl and her dad." I asked no one in particular, but looked at my mom when I spoke. Elena started to protest, but thought better of it when my mom answered, "Of course you can."

In the car I promised Mom and Aunt Inez that I would only go to the Blue Turtle and that they wouldn't have to send out a search party for me. On the way to the gallery I passed a laughing group of five girls walking arm in arm. Oh, major BSG attack. You know, the kind of friendship attack when you really want to hang with your BFFs and you can't. Suddenly I wanted to sit down at Montoya's Bakery, our hangout, for some hot chocolate with my buds and explain the tight situation I was in. Together I just knew we would figure out what to do!

When I first walked into the Blue Turtle, I didn't see anyone. "Xochitl," I called out.

She hurtled in through the big sliding-glass doors. "Isabel! What happened? Did you get grounded for life or what?"

I quickly filled her in, and she seemed relieved that I didn't get into major trouble because of my previous disappearing act.

I saw a large printer on the desk and suddenly had a brilliant idea. "Xochitl, can I ask a favor? One artist to another." She nodded. "I took some photos at the family party the other night, and I'd like to blow them up and print them out. You know, for the party decor. I'll certainly pay for the paper and the ink."

"Sure, we just had a bunch of supplies delivered yesterday. Can I see the pics?" she asked.

I put the camera in display mode and scrolled through the photos. She especially liked the one where I surprised Elena Maria at the pool. "Oooh, that one? All blown up? That'll be majorly funny!"

We went through more of the pictures, giggling at most of them. Suddenly the picture of half the cave art came into view. We both stared, not saying a word. Finally Xochitl spoke up.

"What's that?" she asked with interest.

"Umm, I'm not sure. A funny thing happened to me and my cousin the other night at the ranch. We, uh, we went armadillo hunting and got, uh, held up in the storm. In a cave. Overnight. The horse ran away." My voice got squeakier as I spilled out details. "My mom doesn't know about it yet! I really hope we don't get into major trouble."

Xochitl stared at the photo, openmouthed. I switched to the last one, the photo of the tools and the woven pouch. Her eyes got wider. "Isabel, do you realize what that is?"

"Not really. But the drawing seemed really old, so I didn't want to use my flash on it too much. I made these sketches." I fumbled in my pack for the notebook.

She flipped through it quickly. Once was enough. She snapped it shut. "I can't believe my eyes," she said.

"*Isabel!*" Uh-oh. My mother and Aunt Inez were at the

door already. I ran up to them. I didn't want them to see the drawings.

"I'm not late, am I?"

"Where's the police?" Xochitl joked. I shot her a look that said *Not now!* and she disappeared into the office.

"At least we didn't have to look for you this time," Aunt Inez said, a little sharply. "In any case, your sister has found the perfect pair of shoes and we are ready to go."

I looked at my mother, who was looking at Aunt Inez with a weird expression. I wondered if my mom thought Aunt Inez was being crabby.

I reentered the office to get my things. Xochitl had already transferred the photos from the memory card onto the computer. "Leave everything to me, okay?" she said, handing me back the card and returning to the gallery with me.

Xochitl turned to my mother. "You know, my father is taking me to the Witte Museum today. Is it okay for Isabel to join us? We can take her home afterward."

What did Xochitl have planned? Whatever it was, I wanted in. I spun around. "Please, Mami, it would be so much fun!"

My mother's face softened. I knew that she loved to see me get all excited. "Is that too much trouble? You'll have to drive all the way to the ranch to bring her home."

"No, really," Xochitl said. "My papa won't mind."

"Out of the question," bossy Aunt Inez said. "Come. We must get going."

I couldn't help it. Tears came to my eyes. Xochitl was seriously disappointed too.

"Just a minute, Inez. I think it's okay," Mom said. Xochitl and I broke into cheers.

"Esperanza? This is not a good idea. We have much to do to prepare for the *quinceañera* tomorrow night."

"Inez," my mother said. "I think my Isabel needs to have some fun, away from the teenagers."

"I won't hear of it. I need her there this afternoon because the stylist is coming to practice the hair and makeup for the honor court."

"Inez, I said my daughter can go."

"But Esperanza—"

"*Inez!*" Mom gave Aunt Inez a fiery stare. A surprised Aunt Inez turned around and walked out of the gallery. "I'll get the car," she called over her shoulder.

"Thank you, Mami," I said.

"Thank you, Mrs. Martinez," Xochitl said at the same time.

I gave my mom a kiss on the cheek and walked her to the door of the gallery. As soon as she got into the car, I started grilling Xochitl for the details. "So, what's this place we're going to? Is it an art museum?"

Xochitl laughed at my excitement. I could tell she was pumped about our adventure too. "It's more like a natural history museum. But there is some art there. And actually . . . my dad doesn't know we're going yet. We haven't been in a while, but he loves the Witte, and I'm sure he'll be happy to take us."

As we printed the pictures, she told me more and more about the museum. I couldn't wait!

This Art Rocks

And Xochitl was right, her father *was* happy to accompany us. I liked being with the two of them because they were always joking with each other. I really wished my dad could be here too, joking and laughing.

The museum was located on the edge of San Antonio's famous Brackenridge Park. As we walked in, I immediately noticed some fencing that looked like it was made of wood but wasn't wood.

"That is a type of concrete art called *faux bois,* French for 'false wood,'" said Mr. Guerrero. "One of the most famous *faux bois* artisans was Dionicio Rodriguez, whose work is here in this park and other places all over San Antonio. Today, artisans in San Antonio are still among the most well-known *faux bois* creators. The masons form concrete to resemble logs, split tree trunks, branches. It's a European art form that came to San Antonio by way of Mexico City," Mr. Guerrero continued. "It's in great demand these days."

"My aunt has some of that at her ranch. It's really neat-looking," I said. "And unlike wood, I'll bet it lasts forever."

"Not as long as petrified wood," Xochitl said. "We'll get to see a lot of that at the museum." We exchanged a glance, keeping our secret about the cave art for the perfect moment.

Inside, Xochitl smoothly urged her father on to the exhibit on rock art. My hands got clammy and I almost broke into a sweat as we got closer.

Xochitl rushed me into a room with a long display case. It contained several samples of fiber objects. As I read the descriptions, a cold wave rumbled through me.

The collection of perfectly preserved pouches, nets, baskets, and part of a sandal came from various limestone caves within a very small territory along the Texas–Mexico border known as the Lower Pecos Region. A sign near the center of the exhibit said that the area ranges along the Rio Grande, from the south where it is crossed by the Devil's River, to the north at the junction with the Pecos River. The people who made the items were primitive, according to archaeologists, but the cave art is among the best in the world, and spectacularly well-preserved. The findings were some of the oldest art in North America. And some of the images were more than *four thousand years old*!

My knees felt weak. And it wasn't because of yesterday's dancing. Four thousand years old . . . the words were running through my brain like a message on the Red Sox Jumbotron at home.

"Come on, there's more to see," Xochitl said, yanking me from my spot. "Get ready. Your eyes are going to pop out of their sockets when you see this!"

We entered another room, filled with actual-size reproductions of rock wall art. They were almost identical to what I'd seen in the cave! I started to feel almost the same way I'd felt in the cave too, like the drawings gave off some kind of magical energy rays or something. It just must be the artist in me. I mean, most kids my age wouldn't get so excited about ancient drawings on a wall.

"Oh, there you girls are," Mr. Guerrero said. "I thought you'd pulled a disappearing act on me, too."

"Daddy, you have to see Isabel's drawings of the stuff she saw in a cave at *Los Mitotes*," Xochitl blurted. She immediately regretted it and gave me a sorry look.

I looked up at the ceiling and hoped I would find the right words.

"What are you talking about, *mi' jita*?" he asked. Xochitl did not speak. "What's this about a cave at *Los Mitotes*?"

"Mr. Guerrero," I said, stepping forward and handing him my notebook, "I had, um, well, an adventure in this cave. Night before last." I took a deep breath and told him the whole story about me and Ricardo spending the night in the cave.

"That young Ruiz boy should know better than to take you there. It could have been a dangerous place."

"Actually, we were lucky we were inside when the rain started. It was pretty intense." I shivered.

He nodded thoughtfully. "All right, Isabel," he said. "You two were very lucky things turned out the way they did for you. And I think you probably should tell your mother . . . perhaps after your sister's big celebration. But what does *that* have to do with this?" he asked, indicating the notebook.

I glanced at Xochitl. "Tell him." She nodded at me to continue.

"Well, lucky for us we had a flashlight, and we found something."

Mr. Guerrero's face showed concern. "What was it?" he asked.

"Rock art, daddy. Real rock art!" Xochitl jumped in. "Just like on the walls here!"

"*¡Que demonios!*" he said. "Rock art? That is incredible! Did you find anything else?"

I nodded. "An old woven bag and some sticks with fibers that reminded me of paintbrushes. We tried not to touch anything."

Mr. Guerrero shook his head in amazement. Xochitl grabbed the notebook out of her father's hands. She rapidly flipped to the pages where I'd made some sketches, and put it up to his face. Her father began to focus on it. His eyes got large. Xochitl flipped a page. His eyes became larger. She flipped to another page, where I'd sketched the tall main figure. He finally tore his eyes away from it and looked at me.

"You drew these?"

I nodded. "As many as I could. We counted almost thirty smaller paintings, and then there was this one big one. Here, I have pictures too."

He scrolled through the images on my camera quickly. "Hector Ruiz does not . . . nobody knows about this?"

I nodded. Mr. Guerrero obviously thought this was a big deal. Xochitl began to hop. "Will Isabel get in trouble?" she asked.

His smile crowded the room. "Not for this. But let's get

out of here so you can tell us the whole story. Do you want to see the Alamo?"

"Do I ever!" I cried.

"Good," he said. "We'll drive by. But then we'll go visit the other missions, the Mission San Francisco de la Espada, Mission San Juan Capistrano, and Mission Concepción. Those are the true beauties of the Old Mission Trail."

CHAPTER

13

The Chef Shuffle

When Mr. Guerrero pulled up in front of the ranch at the end of the day to drop me off, I immediately spotted my mom sitting on the front porch and ran to her. Mr. Guerrero and Xochitl followed me onto the porch. "Mom, can we invite Xochitl and her parents to the *quince*?" I begged.

"I think we can arrange that, Isabel." She addressed Xochitl's father. "Cesar, will you and your family please join us tomorrow night for my daughter Elena Maria's *quinceañera*?"

"Certainly, Mrs. Martinez. Xochitl and I would love to meet the honored young lady."

I giggled. I just couldn't help myself. Things were finally looking up, in a big way!

Just then Uncle Hector stepped out onto the porch. "I thought I heard a truck out here. *Buenos tardes*, Cesar. Thank you again for bringing our little Isabel home."

"Ah, Hector. Just the man I was looking for. May I speak

to you for a moment, privately? It is a matter of . . . art."

"Of course, of course," Uncle Hector told him, drawing him to the side of the porch. While the two of them talked, Xochitl and I told my mom all about our incredible day . . . leaving out the part about the cave art. I wanted to find the perfect time to reveal my big discovery to her.

When Uncle Hector and Mr. Guerrero were finished talking, my uncle looked pale, and he gave me a funny look. I knew they must have been talking about the cave. Mr. Guerrero nodded at me, then winked at Xochitl. "Come on, daughter. Time to head home," he told her.

"See you tomorrow!" I called out after her.

Elena Maria met me right inside the door to the house. She smiled sweetly at Uncle Hector as he walked past us and then morphed into *Quince*-zilla again right before my eyes.

"Isabel, Mom told me where you've been all afternoon," she said, stopping me in my tracks. "Do you understand how much work there is to do here? Decorations, favors, cooking, practicing hair and makeup. It's stressing me out just talking about it! I can't believe you would spend the day before my *quinceañera* hanging out with some girl you just met, and not *me*. Your *sister*."

I couldn't believe it. My sister actually missed me. I gave her a big hug while I explained enthusiastically, "She's my new friend, Elena. You'll get to meet her. Mom and I invited her to the *quince* . . . and I know you'll love her."

She was outraged. "You invited some strangers to my

party?" she shouted as she pulled away from me.

"Elena Maria!" my mother said, coming in through the front door. She must have heard our conversation. "Control yourself. The Guerreros are friends of Hector and Inez, and *I* invited them. But Isabel, some of this is true. I'm glad you had fun this afternoon, but now we need to focus on the *quince*. Let's help your sister."

"Mami, Papa just called but we missed him," Elena Maria said, sounding annoyed. "I was in the pool and didn't hear the phone ring. Mercedes answered and told him you were outside, and he told her not to bother us. He said he couldn't actually pin down 'an arrival time.'" Elena Maria sighed. I heard her mumble, "This is the craziest, most mixed-up party ever!"

My mother wasn't even irritated by the news.

"What is going on, Mami?" She pretended that she didn't hear my question.

"Isabel, tomorrow is an important day, one we've all waited for for a long, long time. I hope you both remember to reflect on the spiritual meaning of this celebration. Please, act gracious to everyone, including one another."

I snuck a quick look at Elena Maria, and at exactly the same time, she snuck a look at me. We cracked up. This time we had a real hug. My sister took off to find her friends, who were having a ferocious card game in the billiards room. I could hear the guys giving each other a hard time. "Oooh, you just got slapped with an ace from the Scott-ster." "Oh yeah, well, watch out for this Andy-Attack, comin' at ya! Whoa!"

Mom said she was going to take a little nap, and I went to the kitchen to fix myself a snack. Ricardo was in there, peeling potatoes. He wore a huge white apron tied at the neck and at his waist. Enrique and Fidencia huddled at the stove, having what looked like a tense discussion. The cooks reminded me of the diva chefs from Elena Maria's favorite TV cooking show.

"What's up with the prison chores?" I asked Ricardo.

He shrugged. "Part of my 'consequences' for the cave thing. A couple of minutes ago my dad marched into my room and told me I needed to get down here and help out in the kitchen. Did you tell him about the cave art?" he asked accusingly.

"No! Mr. Guerrero did. He took us to the Witte and I saw the exhibit on rock art they have there. Xochitl told her dad about the art. So I showed him the notebook and the pictures, and then he had this whole private conversation with your dad when he dropped me off."

"Yeah, well, my father also said I put you in 'danger.'"

"He doesn't know how courageous you were. Like capturing the water? I'll tell him the whole story. Then he'll think you're a hero," I assured Ricardo. No matter how goofy he was, I really did feel like he had kind of saved my life. "Anyway, Mr. Guerrero said he would contact some friends of his at the university. He was pretty blown away by our pictures and the sketches. Ricardo." I checked to make sure Enrique and Fidencia weren't listening and told him, "We might have made an important art discovery."

Just then a spoon clattered to the floor. Enrique and Fidencia started to shout at each other.

"More eggs!" she yelled at her husband.

"No. More flour," he countered.

"Eggs!"

"Flour!"

Fidencia stared at her husband with dragon eyes. I was pretty sure smoke was about to come out of her nostrils. "You want more flour? Here is your flour!" With that, she grabbed a whole bag of white flour and dumped it over his head.

I clapped my hand over my mouth and looked at Ricardo, who was wide-eyed behind his glasses. Enrique sputtered and blinked, trying to get the flour out of his eyes. Finally he took off his apron. He hung it on the wall, and said in a most gentlemanly voice, "I am off to Sonora, to stay with my brother. I will return in a month to pick up my things. So have them ready!" Then he walked out.

Fidencia cupped her ample cheeks in her hands. "*Dios mío*!" she exclaimed. She turned to Ricardo and, speaking in Spanish, just as calmly said the following:

"My work is done here. The entire menu is prepared and ready for tomorrow, except for the cake. Bake five individual two-layer cakes, and frost each on the outside with buttercream icing, food coloring to be added at the cook's discretion. For the icing between the layers, I suggest a pineapple-lemon filling."

With that, she dramatically removed her apron and handed it to Ricardo, whose face was now white with shock.

"I will phone my sister in the city and have her pick me up immediately. Please tell Don Hector and Doña Inez it's been a pleasure working here and helping to raise you children for the last ten years. I will settle my salary account in two weeks." She left the kitchen.

Ricardo and I stared at each other. *Dios mío* was right!

"What do we do now?" Ricardo turned to me like I somehow had an answer, which I didn't. "Isabel, you and I have taken a ride on the trouble train this week." Ricardo shook his head.

He was right about that. I didn't want any more trouble—not before my sister's *quince*. I began pacing around the kitchen like a goose being chased by a dog. I flapped my arms up and down and charged every which way. Suddenly I stopped.

"Wait here," I directed Ricardo as I hurried out of the kitchen, on a mission to save my sister's *quince*. I raced down the hall and skidded to a stop outside the billiards room. I found just the person I needed, playing air hockey.

"Got a few minutes, Scott? We have an emergency in the kitchen."

He perked up. "In the kitchen?" I could practically see the gears turning in his brain. Scott wanted to have a TV cooking show when he grew up, and he was already an awesome cook, just like my sister.

"It's a culinary"—my sister taught me that term— "emergency," I explained as we headed out. "Enrique and Fidencia just quit! And we need a cake . . . a *big* cake for the party tomorrow."

"They quit? That's intense. Just now?"

"No kidding. Ricardo and I were just standing there when they started yelling at each other about eggs and flour, then Fidencia dumped flour on Enrique's head!"

"Whoa!" Scott thought about what I'd said. "Wow. And they seemed so happy. Just goes to show you never know. Okay, show me the way." He put on a serious face and said, "Iron Chef Scott to the rescue!" I almost cracked up, but I managed to keep it together. Scott could be as goofy as he wanted, as a long as he baked Elena Maria a fab cake!

Ricardo repeated Fidencia's instructions to Scott, who wrote it down like a reporter covering a news conference.

"Two layers?" he said, surveying the stack of cake pans. "Let's make it four. One *quince* cake, coming up. Isabel, get me some flour, milk, sugar, eggs, lemons, crushed pine-apple, butter, salt, baking powder, vanilla, aaaaaand . . . what else, what else?"

"An apron!" I said, tossing Enrique's apron to him.

By the time I finished putting everything on the big prep table, Scott had rounded up the large electric mixer, spatulas, a timer, measuring cups and spoons, and a box of toothpicks. He was busy scribbling notes on a paper.

"Hmm. We're expecting about a hundred people, wouldn't you say, including the musicians? So, my recipe calculations tell me that for the cake I will need fifteen sticks of butter, fifteen cups of sugar, twenty cups of flour, twenty teaspoons of baking powder, two-and-a-half tea-spoons of salt, two and a half dozen eggs—that's thirty eggs, Isabel—seven-and-a-half cups of milk, and twenty teaspoons of vanilla. And for the frosting, another two-and-a-half cups of milk, six tablespoons of vanilla, seven-and-a-half tablespoons of lemon juice, two-and-a-half teaspoons of lemon zest, twenty-two-and-a-half cups of confectioners' sugar, seven-and-a-half pounds of butter, and . . . are you ready?"

My eyes were bugging from the amounts he'd mentioned.

"Seven-and-a-half pounds of butter!" My mouth fell open, but Scott didn't miss a beat. I was wondering if we were all going to have heart attacks from eating all that butter!

"You measure, I mix. Ricardo, preheat the oven."

We got busy and scuttled around the kitchen to retrieve yet another utensil for Chef Scott. We taught him the Spanish words for the ingredients, and Ricardo answered his many questions about *Los Mitotes* and the cows. Jill and Lauren wandered in, but Scott shooed them out with a flick of his batter-encrusted spatula. When he heard Elena Maria's voice in the hallway, he nearly went into overdrive.

"Out, out! Elena Maria, least of all, should be in here!" he cried. "Isabel, distract her!"

I dashed out the door and almost ran smack into my sister, who was wearing her dress for the party tomorrow. She gave me a funny look. Of course, there was flour in my hair, on my nose, on my clothes . . . it looked like I had taken a flour bath!

"Uh, hey, Izzy. What are you doing in there? I need a snack. I've been practicing my waltz steps in my room, and I'm *famished*."

"Uhhh, you can't go in there!" I said, stepping in front of her.

"Why not?" She crossed her arms.

"Because . . . because . . ." I looked around frantically, trying to come up with a good reason. Suddenly I realized it was standing right in front of me. "Because you're wearing your *quince* dress!"

"So? I have to practice dancing in it to make sure I won't trip or anything."

"But the kitchen is a total mess. Look at me . . . flour everywhere. And Freckles is in there, and he would totally peck your dress to shreds!"

Elena's eyes widened. "Oh, Isabel. You are absolutely right! I can't believe I was about to walk in there in this. What am I thinking?" She shook her head. "This *quince* thing is making me a little *loca*, I think." She gave me a quick kiss on the cheek.

No kidding, I wanted to say, but I didn't, because Elena Maria was being so nice. "In fact, why don't I just get Scott to bring some chips up to your room?" I suggested.

She broke into a grin. "Thanks, Iz. You know what? You're such a sweet little sister after all." She started to turn away, then stopped. "What's Scott doing in there, anyway?"

I gave her a grin the size of Texas and said, "It's a surprise. For you."

"Oh!" She pursed her lips and flounced away down the hall. Avery would be so proud of me. My matchmaking skills had definitely improved.

"Phew!" I breathed a sigh of relief as I popped back into the kitchen. "That was close, Scott! I had to promise her you would bring some chips up to her room."

"No problem," he agreed. "Good work!"

The timers rang. Scott tested the cakes with a toothpick. When it emerged from the pan without a speck of batter, he pronounced them done. We waited for the cakes to cool while Scott made the pineapple-lemon filling. He gave me a taste and I drooled while he got to work cutting and reassembling the cakes.

"*Voilà.* My friends, this is what is known as the first tier."

Scott quickly assembled the second tier, then moved onto the third and final tier. When he was done, he stepped back to admire his work.

"That looks incredible, Scott," I said, clapping him on the back.

"Wow! Did I really do this?"

I nodded. "All you need is the buttercream frosting, and you're done."

"That kind of frosting works best when it's nice and cold. We have to let the cakes thoroughly cool too. Here's what I'll do. I'll make the frosting, let it sit overnight in the fridge, then put the final touches on it tomorrow morning. What do you think, Isabel?"

"Dude—you should have your own TV cooking show for sure. That was awesome!"

CHAPTER

14

Whodunit?

"That was a close one," I said to Ricardo as we stumbled out of the kitchen after spending almost an hour getting everything cleaned up. We were both completely wiped out from being Scott's assistant chefs, on top of the earlier night's adventures in the cave.

"Yeah. That guy Scott can really cook! Good thing he was here."

"What's going to happen with Fidencia and Enrique?" I asked as we headed toward Ricardo's room to chill for a while. "That was so crazy, the way they just quit like that."

"I don't know," he said, shaking his head. "I mean, I've seen them blow up before, but never . . ."

As we passed Uncle Hector's office, we both heard him talking to someone on the phone. "So I need a whole order of your famous *empanadas* for tomorrow, if you can do it. Mmm-hmm. Yep, it's been quite a week around here. First the thing with our housekeeper, and now my cooks walk out on us the day before my niece's *quinceañera!*"

My eyes got huge. I grabbed Ricardo's arm and dragged him into the stairwell before I turned around to talk to him. *"The thing with our housekeeper?* Ricardo, does that mean what I think it means?"

"Uhh . . . what do you think it means?"

"Ricardo!" I could tell he was just pretending he didn't get it because he didn't really *want* to get it. "That means they really do think that Mercedes broke the eagle!"

"How do you know?"

"Didn't you just hear your dad? Come on!" Again I had to practically drag him up the stairs to the hallway that led to Mercedes's room and my room. When we got to the top, we heard voices that were unmistakable. It was definitely Mercedes and Ricardo's mom having a very passionate conversation in Mercedes's room. I looked at Ricardo, he looked at me, and we immediately (and superquietly) dashed past Mercedes's partially open door, slipped into my room, and shut the door.

"Is your mom firing Mercedes right now?" I practically shrieked.

"Shhhh!" Ricardo shushed me. "I don't know!"

I looked wildly around the room until my eyes landed on the glass, cup-shaped candleholder on my little bedside table.

"Perfect!" I snatched up the glass and ran to the other side of the room, pressing the glass to the wall and my ear to the glass.

"What are they saying?" Ricardo asked immediately.

"Shhhh!" Now it was my turn to shush him. "I can barely hear, okay?"

We both held our breath. I listened carefully. They were speaking Spanish, so I had a little trouble figuring out what was going on at first, but then I heard something that sent chills down my spine.

"Doña Inez, perhaps it is fixable?" Mercedes said. "I could try and . . ."

I pulled my ear away from the wall and gasped. "Ricardo, we have to get in there right now! We can't let your mom think that Mercedes broke the eagle."

Ricardo looked more scared than I had ever seen him, even when we were stuck in the creepy cave. He swallowed. "You're right," he said quietly. "Let's go." I was proud of my cousin. It was going to take a lot of courage for him to face Aunt Inez.

I placed the candleholder carefully back on the little table and folded my hands in front of me. This was it. The walk from my room to the room right next door was probably the longest five feet I have ever walked.

"Knock," Ricardo whispered to me when we stood outside the door.

"You knock," I whispered back.

Just as he raised his hand to do it, the door was pulled open. I saw Mercedes sitting on her bed with a worried look on her face.

"I thought I heard you come up, Isabel," Aunt Inez said. "We are having a very important conversation here. I can speak with you two in a minute."

"No—Mom, we really need to talk to you now," Ricardo spoke up.

"Ricardo!" Aunt Inez sounded surprised. "I said I could talk to you in a minute. Please leave us now."

"Aunt Inez, it was me!" I blurted out. Then I froze. Everybody stared at me, including Mercedes.

"What was you, Isabel?" Aunt Inez asked slowly.

"The eagle," I mumbled, looking down. "I broke the eagle. And I'm so so so so really incredibly sorry. I know it was like your favorite piece of art. I can't imagine how I would feel if I had such a great art collection and then someone came in and—"

"It wasn't Isabel, Mom," Ricardo interrupted me. "It was me." My mouth fell open as I turned to look at him. Aunt Inez raised an eyebrow. "I know I'm not supposed to go in there, but I just wanted to show Isabel, and then I picked up the eagle and it just . . . slipped. I'm sorry." He looked at the ground.

I couldn't believe it. Ricardo was covering for me? Why?

"Aunt Inez," I tried again. "That is not the truth. The truth is that *I* broke the eagle."

"No, *I* broke the eagle," Ricardo countered, giving me a glance that meant *Stop talking—now*.

Mercedes spoke up from her place on the bed. "Perhaps . . . could it be . . . that you both had a hand in breaking this eagle?"

Ricardo and I stared at each other. "Yeah," we admitted finally.

Aunt Inez looked at one of us, then the other. "Thank you for your confession," she said simply. I couldn't believe that's all she had to say. I expected a blowup the size of Texas, and we got a thank-you. I would never understand grown-ups. Never.

After a brief pause and an odd look at Ricardo, Aunt Inez turned and nodded at Mercedes. "Regardless of what happened to the bench by the barn, it needs to be fixed in time for the celebration tomorrow. Find Tomás and see if he can do anything for it."

The bench by the barn? Ricardo and I looked at each other in disbelief. Aunt Inez hadn't been accusing Mercedes of breaking the eagle at all. In fact, she didn't even know about the broken eagle. I raised my arms and dropped them to my sides.

"And you two"—Aunt Inez beckoned—"are coming with me."

A few minutes later Ricardo, Aunt Inez, Uncle Hector, and I all stood in a circle around the repaired eagle.

"I am really sorry," I whispered for the forty-thousandth time.

"I know that you are," Uncle Hector told me. "We all make mistakes, Isabel."

"That's right," Aunt Inez agreed. She shook her head at us. "I hope you know now I would never fire a valuable employee—a lovely person like Mercedes—just because she made a mistake."

Uncle Hector nodded and turned to me. "If the story you tell about this accident with our eagle is true, Isabel, then there was really nothing you could have done to prevent it. Except, of course"—he looked sternly at Ricardo—"to not be in this room in the first place."

"I'm really sorry, Mom, Dad," Ricardo repeated, looking from one parent to the other. I felt worse for Ricardo. It's like my poor cousin couldn't get anything right this week.

"Sorry is important, son," Uncle Hector told him, "but you have to learn that there are consequences for your actions. You will be a member of the cleanup crew, bright and early the morning after the *quinceañera*. An *active* member."

"But, Dad!" Ricardo started. "I just got finished with . . ." he stopped suddenly, realizing what he was saying. I realized it too. Ricardo's mom didn't know that we had spent the night in the cave, so she didn't know about the punishment his dad had given him of peeling potatoes in the kitchen. And Ricardo definitely didn't want her to know about any of it now.

"Finished with what?" she asked him, looking puzzled.

"Uhhh . . . nothing. Finished with cleaning my room," he mumbled. He exchanged a look with his dad. I could tell what it meant: *You're safe—for now.*

"I want to be on the cleaning crew too," I volunteered. Ricardo looked at me in surprise. "I mean, I'm the one who actually knocked it over. It's only fair."

"That's very mature, Isabel," Aunt Inez told me. I had to smile at that compliment. Me, mature. I liked the sound of that.

As we walked away I heard her say to Uncle Hector, "How will we ever explain this to Cesar Guerrero?" Oh, no. I shook my head. Mr. Guerrero *was* the artist.

"Ricardo, why didn't you tell me Mr. Guerrero was the artist who sculpted the eagle? How will I ever face him and Xochitl again?"

"I didn't know it was him. Honest, Isabel. My mom just got that piece—she never told me who she bought it from."

Right before we headed to our separate wings of the house, Ricardo asked me, "Why'd you volunteer for the cleaning crew? That was pretty stupid."

I rolled my eyes. Boys were just so clueless about the important things in life . . . like friendship.

"Why'd you say it was you who broke the eagle?" I countered.

He was silent for a minute. "Yeah, okay. Yeah. I get it."

He gave me a thumbs-up and headed off to his room. I smiled too. I guessed that, from a boy, that was as close to "Friends forever!" as I was ever going to hear.

CHAPTER

15

Dreams Do Come True

On the morning of the big day I found Mercedes in the kitchen, frantically trying to assemble breakfast without the help of Fidencia or Enrique. The first thing I noticed was the finished cake. The entire piece was iced in whorls of creamy frosting. Tiny silk flowers were delicately arranged on the various tiers. It looked like something out of a magazine.

"Did Scott do this?" I asked Mercedes.

"*El Señor Scott,*" she answered. "*Magnífico, ¿no?*"

"*¡Sí, sí! ¡Magnífico!*" I repeated. The cake was a work of art!

At that moment Elena Maria walked in, followed by Lauren and Jill. Everybody froze when they saw the cake.

Elena Maria was glued to the spot. "When? How? But who? I thought Fidencia and Enrique quit. . . ."

"I made it. For you, Elena," said Scott, who magically appeared at that moment. "Of course, I had some help from assistant chef Isabel." He ruffled my hair.

The smile on my sister's face could have melted a gla-
cier. She started to cry. Her friends hugged her.

"Scott, this is . . . beautiful. However did you do this?"
she asked.

"With a little *harina, azúcar, huevos,* and *mantequilla.*
How else? Mercedes helped me with the frosting and with
the little flowers. She and Fidencia had planned the cake
together, so the columns, the decorations, everything was
already here," Scott said proudly.

Mercedes beamed. Freckles crowed again and Mercedes took off after him, once more, with a broom. Elena
Maria hugged Scott, who turned all sorts of red.

"Here, sister," I said, handing her an envelope that
contained a hand-drawn birthday card. I had spent a lot
of time making it at home, so I hoped she liked it. "Happy
quince."

"Ooh, nice, Isabel," she said. Lauren and Jill grouped
around her.

"That's so cool!" Jill said.

"You drew this?" Lauren asked.

I nodded. I watched my sister carefully open the envelope and take out the card. She smiled at me, but I could
still see worry in her face.

"Anymore news about Papa yet?" I asked.

She looked up, dejected, and shook her head. "Mom
said he's en route, whatever that means."

I remembered Mom's earlier mysterious smile. "He'll
be here. I just know it." I held her hand and to make her
smile, said, "I will fly on my 'little sister pest' broom to go

and get him if I have to. He's not going to miss his favorite daughter's party. No way!"

She waved her finger at me. It was a little joke between us. Whoever needed Mom and Dad more was the favorite daughter.

We all stood around admiring the cake, when who walked in through the back door but Enrique and Fidencia, holding hands and looking dreamily into each other's eyes! "What a crazy couple," I mumbled.

Fidencia dropped her husband's hand and marched right over when she saw the cake. She examined it as if she was looking for the tiniest flaws.

"Who made this cake?" she asked haughtily.

Scott stepped away from the group.

"I did, Fidencia. I apologize if I invaded your territory, but we didn't think you were coming back. I tried my best to treat your *cocina* with respect." Boy, did Scott have his chef manners down.

The chubby chef inspected the confection one more time. "*Bueno, Señor Scott. Muy bueno.*"

I looked over at Elena Maria. We both knew at that instant that Scott Madden was the perfect *quince* escort for her.

Flowers and Banners and *Animalitos*, Oh My!

After downing two bowls of cornflakes with fresh strawberries, I went to the patio to help with the party setup. I walked into a whirlwind of activity. It seemed all the girls were there to help, from the cousins to the aunts to the grandmothers. Aunt Lourdes, back from her friend's house, had jumped right into the middle of the action—as usual. The only ones missing were Elena Maria, and Lauren and Jill, who had been told to keep my sister away for the entire day.

I saw Mom, Aunt Lourdes, and Aunt Inez huddled in a corner, each of them waving her arms excitedly. As I got closer, I heard the sounds of raised voices.

"Esperanza," Aunt Inez said to my mother, "Don't be unreasonable. I've taken care of all of this so that you wouldn't have to. I so wish you would use this time to relax. You'll need your strength for tonight."

"She's doing better than she has in weeks, Inez," Aunt Lourdes said. "Let her pitch in if she wants to."

"Please, if you just step aside we can get this finished in a couple of hours. I'm only waiting for the flowers to be delivered."

"Inez, listen to me. You've done far too much already," Mom said. "I want to contribute to my daughter's party."

"Nonsense! Hector and I are pleased to give your family this party."

My mother pierced her with a look I recognized: the same one my sister had given me when she was at her wits' end. Even Aunt Lourdes seemed to shrink.

"Enough," my mom announced. "Stop what you're doing right now. I have an announcement to make. My Isabel and I have created some decorations that we need your help in arranging."

Everyone in the room froze and stared at my mom.

Aunt Inez was shocked. Her breath caught. I knew what she was feeling—her artistic vision was slipping through her fingers. But I felt my mother had a right to decorate her own daughter's *quinceañera*. On this one I had to stand with Mom.

"Inez, we will work the flowers into the decor after we've put up what I have here." She pointed to the box. I skipped over, shaking with excitement and trepidation. I was proud of what Mom and I had created, but I didn't want to offend Aunt Inez. She was doing so much to make Elena Maria's party unforgettable.

My two aunts were mystified by the box, which my mom put on a table and opened up. She handed me one end of string and as I walked away, a beautiful banner of *papel picado* unfolded. A collective "ohhhh" escaped from everyone.

"Isabel and I made these. There's more." Mom handed out stacks of the connected tissue squares.

Aunt Inez's demeanor changed from anger to total appreciation. "Oh! These are lovely! I didn't think of doing anything like this! Esperanza, you are so creative." I realized that no matter how bossy my aunt was, she really appreciated beauty and would praise generously anyone who created something "lovely." She really was a patron of the arts.

My mom blushed under her praise. "This isn't all," she said. She opened a second box and dumped the hundreds of folded paper animals, many more than she'd shown me the other night, on the table.

"Tía Esperanza," declared Sonia, "these are like something out of a party catalog." I had to bite my cheeks to keep from laughing at that one.

"Isabel, did you make some of these too?" Alisa asked me.

"Yup!" It made me happy to see my mother take charge.

After everyone finished cooing over our work, Aunt Inez jumped into action.

"*Muchachas*," she said. "Let's hang these up and get the show on the road!"

Dream Party

What happened later went so fast I can hardly remember. All I know is that at some point in the afternoon, I had to go to my room to put on my dress. I had expected the dress, picked out by Aunt Inez, to be way over the top—ruffles, lace, giant puffy sleeves, everything—but it was actually very simple and really pretty. Just my style.

As I twirled around, watching the skirt flare out around me, I noticed that the sun had gone behind a cloud and the walls in my room changed color again. I had to stop and stare for a while. Was it a shade of lavender, or setting-sun pink? *I'll miss this magic room when I'm gone,* I thought. The room I had felt banished to when I arrived turned out to be my sanctuary.

Unlike my peaceful room, Elena Maria's room was a makeover madhouse. She and her honor court reminded me of the squawking chickens that were always running around outside the house.

Jill came after me with ten gallons of styling gel. "I think you need a little more color, Isabel, too," Lauren said, coming at me with all kinds of shiny tools and brushes. Eek! I finally let her put blush on my cheeks and gloss on my lips, but I had to run away from her to avoid eyeliner, shadow, mascara, and brow pencil. I was definitely not ready for a total makeover.

We all gathered at the side of the house before walking to the old barn. The late afternoon sun shot rays through the clouds, which glowed in dazzling shades of peach and purple. I'd never seen such a glorious sunset. At the other end of the darkening sky a pale full moon appeared above the horizon. The land itself had been transformed by the recent rain. Texas bluebonnets blanketed an entire pasture, providing an electric blue contrast to the vivid green grass. I wished I had my sketchpad and almost ran inside to get it—until I saw Elena Maria.

She looked almost unrecognizable to me. Her hair was swept up on top of her head with a ring of tiny white roses, held in place by a beautiful silver and turquoise comb that I immediately recognized—it had been passed down through our family from our great aunt. She wore sparkly dangling earrings, and her face was made up like a magazine model's—thanks to Lauren, I was sure. She was so beautiful. To me, she truly looked like a princess. "Wow," I whispered. Mom squeezed my hand. I'd never seen her with such a huge smile.

We took a deep breath before starting the procession. Everything was ready, except . . . no Dad. Mom, Elena

Maria, and I didn't say anything, but I knew that each of us missed him terribly. His parents, Papa Margarito and Mama Maria, were sad and disappointed. I thought I must have misunderstood Mom's secret smile. I saw a little tear brimming on the corner of Elena's eye. But, just like a real princess, she brushed it away and put on her bravest smile. I was so proud of her.

We walked with Mama Maria, Papa Margarito, and my mother's parents, Abuelito José and Abuelita Juanita. We were followed by the large party that included Elena Maria's friends, the Ruiz family, and several dozen relatives.

The picnic area next to the barn was even more beautiful than Aunt Inez had described it. I recognized the benches and the water fountain as *faux bois*, the concrete formed to look like wood. One of those must have been the broken bench that Aunt Inez was talking to Mercedes about, I figured. It certainly wasn't broken anymore—everything looked perfect. Stone vases full of flowers sat to either side of the benches, and tin buckets with gladiolas of all colors surrounded the fountain.

My mother's cousin, Father Miguel, the priest, was waiting by the huge tree, next to a trellis decorated with flowers and a gauzy white fabric that formed a canopy. Father Miguel greeted us when we reached the trellis, and indicated that all of us except my sister should take a seat at a bench. Elena Maria stepped under the canopy and sat on an old and beautifully carved white chair. I could feel my heart pounding, and all of the beauty wasn't even for me. I imagined how nervous and excited Elena had to feel, sitting up there all by herself.

"Family, friends, youngsters, and beloved elders," Father Miguel began. "Today marks a milestone for my cousin, Elena Maria. Although she lives far away from many of us, she and her family have never been far from our hearts. Many of us have witnessed her growth from infancy to the lovely young woman she is today."

I sneaked a peek at her. My mature sister looked scared to death!

"Elena Maria," he said. "You are now fifteen. For millennia our culture has observed this stage of a girl's life as the moment of passage from childhood to maturity, of being watched over and cared for, to beginning her own journey.

"The ritual we will soon witness has undoubtedly undergone changes over the last hundred years. It will be a mix of traditional customs with modern elements, and it surely will be unforgettable fun! But before we move on to the great *fiesta*, I want to say a few words to my young cousin, words that I hope all of us here will also take to heart."

He looked at her with kind eyes. Elena Maria was spellbound.

"As you cross the divide to adulthood, remember to be true to yourself. Always be kind, and let no one keep you from doing what you believe is right and proper. As you grow into your newfound freedom, never forget that along with it comes responsibility, to yourself, to your family, to the world around you.

"Everyone present is here to support you on this journey. We have faith that you will become a model for others to emulate. And now, please stand, Elena Maria."

She rose, looking a little nervous, but I was so impressed by how graceful she seemed up there. *Way to go, quinceañera!* I cheered in my head.

Father Miguel took her by the elbow and led her away from the trellis. He spoke to her in a voice that was inaudible to the audience. Elena Maria nodded several times, and broke into a smile that got bigger by the minute. Soon they were sharing a laugh. They hugged, and then he placed a gold chain with a ruby heart around her neck.

"Let the dancing begin!" Father Miguel shouted. Everybody rose to head back to the house, but then something incredible happened. Enrique appeared from behind the barn, driving an old-fashioned cart adorned with garlands of paper flowers. Hitched to the cart was Rasquatch, dressed to the nines for the occasion with a top hat on his head and a ring of fresh flowers around his neck. He whinnied and scratched at the dirt with his hoof, causing a flock of robins to explode in flight.

Elena Maria squealed and pressed her hands to her mouth. She had gotten her horse and carriage after all!

I was the first to jump into the back, and found a seat on one of the hay bales. The rest of the honor court followed. "Aren't you going to help me up, Andy?" an indignant Jill complained. Andy turned red as he reluctantly held out a hand to haul her into the cart. I had to bite my lip to keep from giggling out loud. So much for being mature adults now!

Lastly, Elena Maria and Scott sat on the bench behind Enrique. He tugged on the reins and Rasquatch, frisky as ever, started a lively trot back to the house.

The sky to the west was now ablaze with hot reds and oranges. The moon was a pale ivory, and the breeze that whipped through my hair felt fresh and cool. We pulled up to the front of the house and got out of the cart. We posed for photos and waited for the next phase of the celebration.

Suddenly something about my sister caught my eye. She stared in the direction of the gate to the ranch. A red van had turned in and was headed toward us. It kicked up a curtain of dust as it raced to the house, and screeched to a stop when it arrived.

Everybody watched in wonder as the passenger door was thrust open. Elena Maria's best friend from Detroit, Deidre, stuck her head out.

"Are we late for the party?" she yelled.

Elena Maria shrieked and ran to her. More girls tumbled out, all friends from Elena Maria's school back home in Detroit. My heart was in my throat as my eyes searched the visitors. And then I saw him. Dad came from around the front, dressed in a suit and looking like a prince.

"Jorge!" my mother cried, and raced to his arms.

"Papa!" Elena Maria and I yelped in unison. We practically flew up to him.

Standing off to the side, almost unnoticed at first, was

my mother's best friend, Luisa. When Mom saw her she laughed in amazement and gave her a tight hug. It was the happiest moment I'd ever had.

"Jorge, I thought . . ." Mom began.

"We drove all day," Dad explained. "The rain stopped just outside of Tulsa and I drove this rented van like a Nascar speed racer. I wanted to give you a surprise you'd never forget, *mi 'jita!*"

The four of us looked at one another, almost disbelieving that we were together again. Dad hugged us as all the friends and family filed into the great room.

"My *mujeres*," he kept repeating. "I've missed you terribly."

Aunt Inez stepped out of the great room and signaled that it was time for Elena Maria to make her entrance.

Dad tugged on the lapels of his suit. "Okay, girls. Let's roll!"

CHAPTER
16

Starlight, Star Bright

With my mother on my sister's side, and me at my Dad's, we stepped through the doors into the great room. I heard Elena Maria gasp when she saw the decorations. The *papel picado* banners twinkled like stars as the lights passed through the tiny cuts.

Even the table centerpieces looked alive. As the candles in the tall clear vases flickered, the flowers and the little paper animals grouped around them seemed to move.

When Elena Maria caught sight of the photos I'd taken and blown up with Xochitl, she gave me a mischievous smile. I wasn't sure what her reaction would be, but she began to nod. She loved the pictures, and so did her friends. Lucky me! Isabel, personal photographer to the *quince* posse.

The burst of horns and violins from a mariachi band caught me by surprise. The lights went low and a spotlight shone on the four of us. It was time for the shoes and tiara!

I couldn't wait to see how beautiful Elena Maria would look with her new gifts from our parents.

I stepped away as Elena, Mom, and Dad walked to the center of the room, where a chair had been placed. She hugged Dad and sat. The guests cheered and clapped and the music got louder and merrier. Mom stepped forward, removed the ring of roses from Elena Maria's head, and placed a sparkling tiara in its place.

"My dearest firstborn, we wish you the happiest of birthdays. This is *your* night. May it be as unforgettable as the day you came into this world."

Dad stepped forward and kneeled as Mom handed him a satin bag with shoes. He removed Elena Maria's flats, then took out a pair of delicate silk shoes with a modest heel. They were perfect! Elena Maria's eyes opened wide and she gave him a huge grin.

"May every step you take get you where you dream of going, no matter what you've got on your feet. Keep your eyes wide open, and just follow the signs," he said.

With the grace of an elegant prince, he placed a shoe on either foot. Elena Maria looked down at him, beaming. "I never knew you had such good taste, Dad!" she told him. Everyone laughed.

"And now, I get the first dance," he said to the crowd.

The band started up. Dad took her hand and, as the music got going, the pair began to dance as if they'd practiced together for weeks.

When it was over, the two bowed to each other, and then to the audience. The mariachis played in the background as Elena Maria, followed by Mom, Dad, and me, stopped at each of the tables to say hi to the guests. I was afraid this part was going to be really boring, but I actually started to have a great time chatting with all our relatives.

The grandmas and grandpas sat together. Papa Margarito pinched my cheek, hard. Mama Maria and Abuelita Juanita cornered me. "So you are liking your new school in Brookline?" they asked.

I thought for a second, then told them, "I'm very lucky, because I have a close-knit circle of friends. There are five of us—Charlotte, Katani, Avery, Maeve, and me." I counted on my fingers. "And we watch out for each other. They've helped me feel less lonely. But I miss all of us living with Papa."

Abuelito José spoke up. "I am grateful my daughter has two wonderful daughters of her own to help her," he said to me.

Papa Margarito nodded. "Jorge is a good son and father. I'm proud of him. But I'm most proud of Esperanza. She's shown tremendous courage during this difficult time."

"Oh, Margarito. Thank you," my mother said, as she clasped his hand.

Mama Maria turned to my mother's parents. "You two have raised a remarkable daughter. I give thanks every day that my son Jorge has such a precious woman as his wife." Then she took my hand. "You're growing up fast, *muchachita*. Soon you'll be exchanging *your* sandals for a pair of pumps. I know you'll be ready."

"Thank you," I whispered, echoing my mom. Mama Maria's words made me feel more grown-up already.

The mariachi band was done. I watched a whole bunch of musicians set up instruments on a stage area in the corner, and was amazed by the variety of instruments: guitars, drums, keyboard, horns, and, perched on a stand, a huge red accordion. Ricardo's accordion! Was he going to play with the band? He hadn't said anything to me about it.

Suddenly it was time for Elena Maria's court to perform the *vals*—our waltz. The background noise of people laughing and talking quieted. I took my place at the end of the line next to Ricardo. I wanted to ask him about the accordion, but that would have to wait. All eyes were on us.

The girls truly looked like damsels from a royal court. Our dresses were cinched at the waist and our skirts swayed gracefully with every step. As part of his *padrino*'s duty, Uncle Hector had outfitted the boys in a neat Western style. Each of them wore a long coat with tails over pressed white shirts. A fancy string tie and gleaming black leather cowboy boots completed the look. They all looked great, but I was feeling way nervous. Would everyone remember the dance I taught them? Would Elena Maria even like it?

The band began to play, and the waltz music began. When the right note sounded, it was showtime.

Ricardo and I started the march, slightly swaying side to side as we moved to our spot on the dance floor. Every fourth step the couples stopped and did the steps I taught them, with perfect timing. Not one dancer was out of place. I caught sight of Elena Maria—she looked thrilled at my surprise addition to the waltz! I felt so proud I thought I would burst. When we were all in place, Elena Maria and Scott moved to the center.

Scott looked tall, sharp, and ready to show off. He took Elena Maria's hand and with all the skill of a seasoned dancer, whisked her around the floor. The two of them glided so easily you could have mistaken them for a pair of ice dancers. I guessed that he was a lot more confident after experiencing my superior dance counsel!

The crowd clapped. They were a hit! Elena Maria looked as if she could not believe this was Scott dancing with her. I couldn't believe it was him, either! At the end of the song he gave her a final twirl. She tripled her spin, and when he caught her they were face-to-face, definitely an unplanned move. Elena Maria was unsure of what to do next, but Scott took charge. He put an arm low around her waist, and *dipped her*. They must have snuck off and practiced together. Note to Avery!

"Way to go, Scott!" I shouted. Elena Maria finally straightened up and the two faced the crowd and took a bow. The applause nearly drowned the cheers. They took another bow, then Scott raised his arm, stepped away, and gave Elena Maria the spotlight all to herself.

She waited to speak until the crowd stopped whooping. The party had hardly begun and everybody was having a fabulous time.

"I want to thank each and every one of you who traveled so far to be here. It means so much to me and my family," she said. "Uncle Hector, Aunt Inez, Tony, Fonzie, Ricardo—your hospitality is bottomless. Thank you so much. I love you all.

"Isabel," she said unexpectedly. "Will you please come here?"

I was nervous. What could she possibly want? I stood next to her, with the bright lights on me. I was so not like my friend Maeve. Being in the spotlight made me nervous. As I walked forward I nibbled at my lips. All I kept thinking was, *Don't trip. Please don't trip.*

She brought out a basket and slowly took something out of it. It was a doll! My favorite part of the *quince* was here. It was really happening to me—my sister was giving me her last doll. I almost fainted, it was so beautiful. Dressed in a traditional folkloric dress from Mexico, the doll looked like a piece of art. Her hair was braided and wrapped with ribbons and piled on top of her head, just like my idol, Frida Kahlo.

"This is for you, *hermanita,*" Elena Maria said as she handed it to me.

My hands shook a little as I held it. This was no ordinary doll.

"Thank you, Elena Maria," I said. I was so overwhelmed that it came out in a whisper. I hugged her tight, but not too tight, so I didn't mess up her dress and tiara. I knew then that I would always be in my sister's heart, and she would be in mine.

Feast for a Princess and Her Court

A long table for Elena Maria's honor court and all our grandparents was set at one end of the dance floor. The place had been magically transformed.

The food table reminded me of an old-fashioned feast. Fidencia's hard work had really paid off. I counted at least eight main dishes: red enchiladas, green enchiladas, chicken in a spicy mole sauce, barbecued steak, short ribs, chicken, tamales, chicken-stuffed flautas, and more.

Some side dishes were so colorful they looked like candy. A large rice dish resembled the Mexican flag. The rice was arrayed in three stripes, green, white, and red. A sprig of parsley in the center made for a perfect national emblem.

This was the greatest family reunion ever. I almost cried to see my father and mother seated next to their parents. All six of them looked so happy. My sister, surrounded by friends she hadn't seen in months, was in heaven.

"Isabel, would you like to help me?" my father asked.

"Yes, Papa, whatever you'd like."

"Please ask one of the musicians for a cordless microphone. I'll need one to make my speech." He removed a crumpled sheet from his jacket pocket.

I skipped over to the youngest musician, who was wearing a shiny gray suit. He looked sharp from his shoes to his head.

He saw me coming and smiled. I thought I saw his brilliant white teeth actually flash a sparkle. He could have been a movie star from one of those old classic movies Maeve is always watching.

"Do you need help?" he asked. His English was perfect.

"My sister's the *quince*. I'm a *dama* in her court of honor," I explained.

"You two look so much alike."

"Thank you," I said. If I looked like Elena Maria did tonight, then I was looking good! "My father is about to make a speech. He asked if he could borrow a microphone."

"Of course." He removed the mike from the stand and pointed to a button. "Just switch this to the 'on' position, and he'll be heard for miles around. Got it?"

"Got it. Thanks. Is this your band?"

"*Sí*. I am Ruben de la Rosa. Do you like this music?" I was captivated by his eyes, which were so deeply hazel-colored they looked almost golden.

"Yeah! I love to dance. What instrument do you play?"

He pointed at his throat. "This is my instrument. I'm the lead singer."

"Who's going to play the accordion?" I asked.

"That belongs to Hector Ruiz's son, Ricardo. He is a star pupil at the local Conjunto Heritage Workshop. I've asked him to sit in with us tonight."

"Cool!" I said. "I thought I recognized that accordion. Rico's my cousin."

I ran back to the table and told my mother. "I just talked to the lead singer of the band!"

"You were talking to the world-famous Ruben. He's the most famous musician in all of Mexico right now. Like a total rock star," she whispered.

"How did they get him to come here?" I asked.

"He's somebody's cousin once removed." She winked. I stared at my mom for a second, then we both burst out laughing. She gave me a hug. "Oh, my. Get ready, my dear. There will be dancing till dawn!"

CHAPTER
17

Dizzy Izzy

Friends, family, neighbors," Dad began his speech. "May I have your attention, please? First of all I'd like to thank all of you for coming. The occasion of my elder daughter's *quinceañera* is most special to me. Thanks to my in-laws for coming all the way down from Detroit, and to my parents for making the long trip from Mexico City to Texas." He held a wineglass up to them. "*Salud,*" he said.

"*¡Salud!*" the crowd shouted.

"Next I'd like to shine the spotlight on my *hermana,* Inez, and her dear husband, Hector." I thought I saw tears well in my father's eyes.

"Inez and Hector, through thick and thin, through good times and hard, you've always been there for my family. We are having an unforgettable time here. On behalf of Esperanza, Isabel, Elena Maria, and her friends, who through your generosity were able to participate, we say *salud*!"

The crowd echoed him. "*¡Salud!*"

"Lastly, to my first baby, *mi muñequita*, Elena Maria." He raised his glass again. The audience got to their feet. "I wish you all the love, peace, and prosperity you deserve. We love you, *mi amor. ¡Salud!*"

Everybody stood and repeated his toast. Elena Maria wiped a tear from her eye, and took the microphone from Dad.

"Thank you, Papa. I want to give a big shout-out to my Aunt Inez and Uncle Hector. This party rocks! I never dreamed I would be surrounded by so much family and so many friends. I love you all very much. Thank you, thank you, thank you," she said.

"But more than anything, I would like everybody to know what an incredible mom I have. Mami, you've made all my dreams come true." She blew a kiss in our mother's direction. "One more thing. You," she said, meaning me, "stand up."

I gulped and got to my feet slowly. She'd already given me the doll. What was this all about? "My little sister, Isabel, helped my mom make these wonderful paper decorations. She's also responsible for putting a lot more drama into our stay here in Texas than I ever imagined. But she's been at my side since I started planning for this event. Thanks for the being the best little sister ever!"

I ran to her side. We collapsed in a hug. The crowd whooped, cheered, and clapped, and she whispered into my ear, "We did it!"

"Now let's have a party and dance!" she shouted to

the room. Ruben the bandleader signaled, and a fanfare followed me to my seat. The band broke into a beat and he let out such a spirited howl, a *grito*, it gave me goose bumps. Just about everybody in the house stood up, raced to the floor, and starting dancing. The room was instantly in high-volume party mode. I spotted my sister and all the *damas* dancing and jumped from my chair to join them.

Thick in the middle of all the dancers, I was surrounded by familiar faces. I saw my cousin Irma, who only recently had been a *quince* herself. The *chambelanes* just had to show off and form a line. They were doing great! I saw Ricardo at the far end of the line, dancing by himself. It suddenly occurred to me that Ricardo spent a lot of time alone.

The music seemed to get wilder and wilder. And just when I thought the song was over, the singer let out another wild *grito*. The dancing crowd seemed to lift off the ground with each new round. I thought I might float away into the night.

Suddenly I spotted two people at the door. Xochitl! I got there in time to catch the end of a conversation between Mr. Guerrero and my aunt and uncle. Uh-oh. Would they tell him about the broken statue? Ricardo must have been thinking the same thing, because he showed up in a flash too, standing next to me with his shoulders all hunched up.

"Ah, here they come!" Mr. Guerrero handed me my sketchpad, and Xochitl shot me a huge grin. The sketchpad was wrapped in a lovely cloth bag. "As I was saying, Mrs. Ruiz, the discovery by these two kids is nothing short of astounding. The photos and the evidence in Isabel's notebook clearly indicate a connection to the ancient Lower Pecos Valley people, perhaps an errant clan. This is the first time evidence like this has been found so far east of the Rio Grande."

Ricardo and I stared at each other. "Wowwwww," was all we could say. Ricardo straightened his shoulders and puffed out his chest with Mr. Guerrero's praise.

"I don't understand," Aunt Inez said. "You're saying that my Ricardo and Isabel made an important archaeological discovery on our property? And you were aware of this?" she asked her husband.

Uncle Hector nodded. "The kids had to find shelter, Inez. They holed up in the cave by the swimming hole after Rasquatch left them stranded during the storm."

"*Dios mío*," she said, losing her balance. "Ricardo, explain."

He gulped. "I invited Isabel to go armadillo hunting. We saddled up on Rasquatch. We went to see the swimming hole, but lightning struck and the horse ran off. We had to find shelter, so we hid in a cave I knew about up there."

"A cave!" Aunt Inez gasped. "Heaven help us, weren't you terrified, Rico?"

"No, Mom. We were pretty lucky to be in there when the rain started. It was a real gully washer. We could have been swept away!"

"Say what?" I cut in. "You never said anything to me about that!"

"It's true, Isabel," Ricardo said, a little sheepishly. "I

just didn't want you to get any more scared." Wow. Ricardo was truly brave. "We had a flashlight, so we went exploring. Isabel saw it first. Pictographs, Mom, lots of them. Shamans and animal pictures!"

"Ricardo was very resourceful, Aunt Inez," I assured her.

She started to fan herself. "*Ay, mi 'jo.*"

Mr. Guerrero intervened. "You'll be hearing from the university this week. The site must be secured immediately."

Uncle Hector patted Ricardo on the back. "Son, I hope this escapade has taught you a lesson. Never again leave on horseback without telling someone. It was a frightening thing for a father to find a riderless horse at the crack of dawn."

"The crack of *whaaat*?" Aunt Inez cried. "How long were you two stuck in the cave?"

"From sundown to sunup," I said. "But Uncle Hector and Enrique rescued us before everyone else was awake."

"Can you show us where you found all of this?" Mr. Guerrero asked us.

"Absolutely!" I said.

"Tomorrow," Uncle Hector told us. "Mr. Guerrero, I hope you won't mind coming out to the ranch again tomorrow. I think there is something else my son and my niece should speak to you about," he said, looking at us meaningfully.

I gulped and looked at Ricardo. That could mean only one thing. Uncle Hector wanted us to tell Mr. Guerrero that we had broken his beautiful eagle statue!

Ricardo, Xochitl, and I needed no more excuse to disappear into the party. We made our getaway as the adults circled in on Aunt Inez.

We found a quiet corner at a table far from the music and the dancers.

"Isabel, my dad has always believed that there was once ancient Indian activity around here," Xochitl said. "I've never seen him so excited. And he was so impressed with your sketches too."

Now I felt really awful. I couldn't hold it in anymore. "Xochitl, I have to tell you something . . . something really terrible," I said. Ricardo kicked me under the table, but I ignored him.

"Yeah? What is it?"

I took a deep breath and spilled the whole story of breaking the eagle her dad sculpted, ending with, "And we're so so so sorry. It was just an accident. A stupid accident."

Xochitl was silent.

"Really sorry," Ricardo repeated softly.

"Welll . . ." Xochitl said slowly. "Now that you told me that . . . actually, I have something to say too." I looked at Ricardo. What could it be? "You remember your beautiful bird sculpture that you made the first day we met, Izzy? That I said I would fire for you?"

"Yeah."

"Well, I fired it for you all right. And then when I was taking it out of the kiln . . . crash. I just dropped it, and it completely shattered. I take things out of there all the time, and that has never happened to me!" She looked at me with big, sad eyes. "So I'm sorry too."

I don't know why, but I just started to giggle. And giggle. At first Xochitl and Ricardo looked at me like I was crazy, but then they started laughing too. We all laughed so hard, we almost couldn't breathe. I was spurting spit out of my mouth, Ricardo was snorting, and Xochitl was holding her stomach.

"I know it's not really funny!" I managed to squeak out.

"But in a way it is," Xochitl agreed, catching her breath. "When things get really bad, it's like, sometimes you have to just laugh or get sick, you know?"

"I feel soooo much better now that I told you," I confessed.

"Me too!" she agreed.

"Me three," Ricardo said. "But the hard part's going to be telling your dad, Xochitl."

"That's tomorrow," Xochitl said firmly. "This party is really rockin', guys. This band is the best. They play it all: ballads, polkas, blues, *rancheras*, a little bit of rock, a little bit of country-western."

"Ricardo's going to play with them later. That's his accordion up there," I said.

"Get outta here! You play?" she asked.

"A little," he said shyly.

"I can't wait to hear you, Rico. I'll bet you're way better than you let on," I teased.

"What's everybody waiting for?" Xochitl said, jumping up. "Let's hit the dance floor."

The three of us wriggled our way to the edge of the stage. We were about to hit our stride when the song abruptly ended.

Ruben pointed his raised fist in Ricardo's direction. "Ricardo, come on up here, man," he said smoothly.

"Ladies and gentleman, we have a special treat for you tonight," the singer said. He had the audience in the palm of his hand.

"We are thrilled to be playing for you tonight at Miss Elena Maria Martinez's *quinceañera*. However, we'd like to depart from our usual repertoire and invite a young man to join us. His name is Ricardo Ruiz. This is his daddy's ranch we're all dancing at. He also happens to be a rising star with the Conjunto Heritage Workshop in San Antonio, an exceptional institution that works tirelessly to preserve our fine musical tradition."

Xochitl and I practically pushed Ricardo onstage. He looked like he was going to throw up.

"Why don't you tell the good folks here something about this music you and so many other young adults are trying to keep alive?"

Ricardo had his big, red accordion strapped over his chest. He stretched the bellows a few times, eliciting a few chords, then spoke into the microphone.

"Uh, thank you for the introduction," he said, shuffling his feet. "I play the accordion." There were some giggles in the crowd, and Ricardo stopped talking.

Ruben took the microphone back from him and stepped in to rescue the situation. I liked this rock star from Mexico! ". . . which in our culture is mostly associated with conjunto music, a style that is unique to the Texas–Mexico border. Conjunto is genuine folk music, the music of the people of the fields. It's made for dancing, especially after a hard day's work. Its popularity has come and gone a couple of times, but right now, we want to ensure it never goes away."

With a two-three count the band was on, this time with the accordion's resonant backbeat. Xochitl and I fell in with the swirling dancers, moving to the rhythm. The floor was crowded. Where had all these people come from? Off to the side I could see Aunt Inez dabbing at her eyes as Ricardo played his heart out. She looked so proud of her son.

Round and round we went. We were almost carried along by the energy of the spinning couples. I was transported by the sounds and the sights. Things were getting blurry, I was getting dizzy, the music got louder, and I just couldn't stop dancing! Maeve, the dancing queen of the BSG, would be out of her mind by now if she were here.

Xochitl and I were by the stage again. Something got in my way and I almost tripped. I looked down just in time to see a flap of feathers and a chicken leg escape the crush of feet.

Oh, no! Freckles had wandered onto the dance floor!

Ricardo saw it too, but didn't miss a beat. At that moment a tornado passed by Xochitl and me. We turned to see Mercedes, broom in hand, chasing Freckles off the dance floor. Amazingly, his squawks could be heard above the music. Hilarious! I could not wait to tell the BSG about this.

When we got tired of dancing we ran into the yard. The evening was just as beautiful away from the noise and the lights. Ricardo joined us after his last number. The three of us played horseshoes in the starlight. We trooped through the kitchen to see the cleanup in progress, but got out of there before they could hand us aprons.

It was past midnight when we grabbed some sodas from the fridge and went to the art-filled living room. Xochitl had asked to see the state of her father's sculpture, but Ricardo and I wouldn't go any farther than the doorway this time.

"Well, you can't really tell from here," she said. "That eagle looks as noble as ever."

That made me feel a little better. "Your dad is an awesome artist, Xochitl. I hope someday I can do something even one-tenth as beautiful as this."

"Girl, by the looks of your drawings, I'd say you're on your way," she answered.

And before we could get ourselves in trouble again, we ran from the room back to the party.

CHAPTER

18

So Late It's Early

Even though Xochitl and her dad had left hours ago, and Ricardo admitted exhaustion and had gone to bed, I was still hyper beyond human capacity. The party was definitely over, but Mom and her best friend, Luisa, sat alone at a table, catching up. I wondered if Mom was tired, and got an idea.

A few minutes later I showed up, pushing the wheelchair Uncle Hector had provided for Mom.

"How did you know I could use a lift?" she asked. "My Isabel," she said to Luisa. "She's my wonderful helper." I leaned into her. She put her arm around my waist as they continued to talk quietly.

Ever since I was a little girl, I loved sitting with my mother and her best friend. I'd listen in on their conversation, amazed by how the two old friends never seemed to tire of each other. I thought of the BSG, back in Brookline. I was one hundred percent certain we'd all still be friends when we were my mom's age.

Elena Maria came to say good night. Her friends had long since gone to bed, tucked in sleeping bags crammed head to toe.

"I couldn't sleep without saying good night . . . and thanking you," she said as she hugged Mom.

She pulled up a chair. Luisa reached for the necklace Father Miguel had given to Elena. "This is lovely, Elena Maria," she said.

"Thank you," she started to say, but was interrupted by a wide yawn.

"Go to sleep now, *mi 'jita.*" My mom laughed.

Elena nodded. "*Buenas noches,* ladies," she said. As I watched her float off to her room, I wondered how long it would take her to come down to earth.

"I think it's time for you and me to turn in, as well," Mom said, looking over at me.

"I'll help," I said, springing into action and bringing the chair around.

Mom was tired, I could tell. Luisa held my mother's arm and steadied her into the seat. She stopped me before we rolled off. "Isabel, I am so proud of the Martinez family. I can tell that you and your sister have matured during your stay in Brookline. Despite the separation from your father and your friends and your school, the two of you have managed to stay happy. You must be very comforting to your mother."

How could I tell her that she had it all wrong? "It's Mom who's been the comfort to us. Elena Maria and I were kind of nervous about living with Aunt Lourdes. She can be a little strict sometimes. But whenever I feel lost in Boston, all I have to do is come home and Mom is there, and I don't feel so alone anymore. She's one strong mom!"

"Oh, sweetheart!" Mom said, and started to cry.

"*Que bonito,*" Luisa said. Her eyes and nose turned red. She cried too.

"Why's everybody crying? Life is good for us. ¿*Verdad, Mami?*"

Mom and Luisa locked eyes and nodded to each other.

"Yes, it is, my dear. Oh my, such wisdom from such a young girl!"

"No." I laughed. "I'm just telling it like it is."

Both of gave a little wave to Dad, who was talking with Aunt Inez, as we left the party and headed for Mom's room. When we got there, Mom and I chatted for a few more minutes.

"When Papa popped out of that van I just about fainted!" I told my mom. "I knew he had something up his sleeve, but what a surprise! Bringing so many of Elena Maria's friends to the party was brilliant. And bringing Luisa, too. He really pulled a fast one."

"That he did, sweetheart."

"How long is Papa staying?" I asked.

"Luisa and the girls are flying back the day after tomorrow. Your papa will leave the same day we do."

"Hurray! It's been so fun hanging out with all our family this week."

"*Ay, mi hijita,*" Mom said with a sigh. "Although for

a minute there, things got a little touchy between me and your Aunt Inez."

"Maybe you were just tired, Mom."

"No, honey. I think it was more than that. I was confused by my feelings. But I think that perhaps I was . . . a bit resentful of her?"

My mom? Resentful? It was so weird to think of grownups feeling that way.

"The way she took control of everything. She didn't even consult me on the menu! Sometimes I felt like I wasn't even the mother of the *quince*. Oh, Isabel, just listen to me. Inez did everything she could to save me from all this work. There is no way I could have done even half of what she did. I'm envious, that's what it is, and I should be grateful. I *am* grateful. Inez deserves all the credit. Please don't tell your sister this, but I'm so glad this is over. Now we can all sit back and just be *family*."

A flashbulb suddenly went off in my head. I had been a little jealous of my sister and her friends!

"Mom, I have a confession too. I was resentful too. Elena Maria called me an attention hog the other day. I was pretty mad about it. But I think she was right, some of the time. I think my problem was that I didn't like *sharing* her so much with her friends. Sometimes I think we've gotten superclose from living in the same bedroom, and then there are times when I think I just don't know her at all."

Mom looked at me sympathetically. "Oh, my dear. It's hard to let go, but that's what we must begin to do with teenagers. Soon you'll be a teenager too." She smiled. "We all want our relatives—our parents, our sisters, brothers, aunts, uncles, and cousins—to be perfect, don't we? But that's not life, *mi amor*. So don't be too hard on yourself. Never forget that it takes a lifetime to really learn to fly."

What she said sounded like something that I knew would make a great caption for one of my cartoons one day. "I'm going to quote you on that, Mom." I kissed her on the forehead and yawned.

Minutes later, I lay snuggled up in my charming room once again. My mind raced over the evening's events. Everything seemed like a movie dream: the incredibly huge oak tree and the sunset, the gorgeous decorations, the mariachis and the flawless dance by the honor court, Scott's cake, armadillos. I felt so far from Brookline and Abigail Adams Junior High.

Just below my window, Freckles shrieked, "Cock-a-doodle-doooooo." I couldn't believe it was so late at night that it was actually morning! The sun would soon be up. I glanced at the family photo by the candle on the night-stand and drifted off to sleep.

CHAPTER
19

The Eagle Soars

Ricardo ran into the great room just as I was reaching to take down the last string of *papel picado*. It made me a little sad to see all the pretty *quinceañera* decorations folded and put into boxes, but I felt lucky that undecorating was my only assigned job on the "cleaning crew."

"Isabel! Xochitl and Mr. Guerrero are here!" Ricardo cried. "I just saw them getting out of his truck!"

I was down off the ladder in two seconds flat. "You remember the plan, right?" he asked as we raced out of the room. We wanted to show Mr. Guerrero the cave where we found the art, get him to drop us off back at the house, and maybe he'd be gone before Uncle Hector even knew the Guerreros were here!

Ricardo and I had said "I'm sorry" so many times this week, we were apologized-out! We just didn't have one more "I'm sorry" left. We figured it would be better to write Mr. Guerrero an apology letter . . . a very nice apology letter. I even planned to include one of my cartoons.

Unfortunately, as we skidded out into the dusty front yard, I saw that we were too late. Uncle Hector was shaking hands with Mr. Guerrero already and inviting him into the house.

"What now?" Ricardo whispered to me. I gulped.

"It's face-the-music time," I said.

Xochitl dashed over to greet us. "Hey, guys! Rockin' party last night. Thanks for the invite."

"No prob," I assured her. "You didn't tell your dad about the statue yet, did you?"

Xochitl's face fell. "No. I hope he doesn't get too mad at you."

"Me too."

Uncle Hector called out to us. "Kids! Head on into the house. We'll meet you in the living room. Ricardo, turn on the lights for the collection, please." We all looked at one another solemnly, knowing what that meant. We marched into the house like a line of prisoners, staring at the floor. I was trying to blink back tears. I could see the headlines now. ISABEL MARTINEZ DESTROYS PRICELESS WORK OF ART.

As Mr. Guerrero followed Uncle Hector into the living room, I saw his eyes scanning the room. They stopped on the glass eagle statue, glowing under the lights. He smiled and started to walk toward it, then stopped. He frowned. He stepped forward slowly until he reached it. Stretching one of his huge hands forward, he ran his finger gently over the seam where we'd glued the wing tip back on.

This was just too horrible to watch, so I buried my face

in my hands. I felt Xochitl slip her arm around my shoulders.

"So that is the issue, Cesar," Uncle Hector said from the doorway. "And I think these two have something to say to you."

"It was my fault, Mr. Guerrero," Ricardo offered boldly. "I'm sorry."

"Me too," I added softly, peeking out from between my fingers.

Mr. Guerrero turned around to face us, and to my surprise, he had a small smile on his face. I raised my head. "And were you also the ones who did the repair work?" he asked.

I nodded.

"Well done, Isabel. If I did not know this piece so well, I might not even have noticed the chip." Xochitl squeezed my shoulders encouragingly.

"Th-thanks," I spit out. I couldn't believe it. He didn't hate me?

"Let me tell you two a story," he began. "It is said that the sculptor Michelangelo's greatest desire was the impossible: not just to imitate life in stone, but to actually create it. And finally, one day, he carved a statue of Moses that was so realistic, so lifelike, that it seemed to him he must have finally achieved his goal. He approached his work and spoke to it. 'Why don't you speak?' he commanded the stone. Yet the statue, being nothing more than rock, would not move. After several minutes he grew so frustrated that it would not answer him, he threw his hammer and chisel at it, breaking a chip off the knee. If you go to see the statue of Moses in Rome, you can see the small damage.

"So," he said as he finished, running his finger again over the tip of glass eagle's wing, "I am in good company. The very best."

We all stood there, staring at the statue. Finally Xochitl broke the silence. "Good story, Dad," she told him. "*Now* can we see the cave art?"

Everyone laughed. "You are a forgiving man, Cesar," Uncle Hector commented. "My wife was very upset when she saw the damage to this piece. It's one of her favorites."

"Well, I'm glad she enjoys it so much. And it's no trouble to be forgiving. Unlike Michelangelo, I love my statues, but I love the living and the breathing more. That's where my art comes from." He looked at Xochitl, Ricardo, and me. "Now, as Xochitl says, let's get on to real reason we came out here today."

We all filed into the hallway and headed for the front door again.

"Your dad is really cool, Xochitl," Ricardo told her.

"Yeah, I guess he is," she said thoughtfully.

"No, really. You're so lucky," he went on. There was that word again. "Lucky." The word Ricardo didn't like when I said it about his family. What was in Ricardo's mind? I wondered.

Suddenly, we rounded a corner and came face-to-face with my mom and Aunt Inez, arm in arm, having a laughing fit as they walked down the hall. It looked like they definitely weren't arguing anymore. My dad was walking right behind them.

"Oh!" my mother exclaimed, out of breath. "Inez, I didn't know you were expecting visitors. Jorge and I wouldn't have kept you chatting in the kitchen with us."

"We're here because of your daughter's amazing discovery, Mrs. Martinez," Mr. Guerrero told her. Ricardo and I exchanged looks.

"Discovery?" my mother asked, sounding puzzled. *Here we go again,* I thought. What would this be, confession number twelve? By now I so over being nervous about telling anybody anything that I spoke right up.

"Yep. I'm so sorry I didn't tell you, Mami. I reeeeally wanted to, but we didn't think it would be a good idea to worry you before the *quince.*"

"Tell me what, *mi 'jita?*"

"That . . . Ricardo and I spent the night that it rained so much in a cave by the *tinaja,* and we found this amazing cave art that's probably thousands of years old."

"*What?!*" my dad and mom said at the exact same time. It looked like my mom was going to faint. Good thing Aunt Inez and Dad were right there to support her. "¡*Dios mío!* You spent the night in a cave? And what is this about art? Will someone please tell me what is going on here?"

"Let's go into the living room," Aunt Inez suggested calmly.

❖ 209 ❖

CHAPTER

20

The Whole Truth and Nothing but the Truth

We all trooped back to the living room and settled in on the big, comfy leather couches while Ricardo and I told my parents everything, from breaking the eagle to our ride on Rasquatch to the creepy cave and the incredible art.

"And believe me, Ricardo has learned his lesson about putting others in dangerous situations," Uncle Hector assured my parents when we were done. Ricardo's face instantly went from excited, telling my parents and the Guerreros all about the armadillos we saw, to frowning, just like that.

"That's right," Aunt Inez continued. "And he knows he is not to come into this room by himself anymore under any circumstances. Isn't that right, Ricardo?"

"You know, I'm not a little kid, Mom," Ricardo retorted. Aunt Inez's mouth formed a perfect O. Everyone was so surprised at Ricardo's outburst, we didn't know what to do. He didn't seem to notice, though. "You think you know everything about me, but you don't know anything! All you guys care about is your expensive art and giving fancy parties and landscaping the patio! You didn't even care when I played my accordion at the *quinceañera* last night!"

We all sat in embarrassed silence. So that was why Ricardo didn't like to talk about all the cool stuff his family had. He thought his parents did waaaay too much talking about it already.

Finally Aunt Inez spoke. She sounded a little choked up. "I noticed, Rico," she said softly. "I noticed when you played. I thought you sounded lovely."

He was quiet for a while too. "Really?" he said.

"Of course," she told him, coming over to wrap him in a giant hug. I could see his face turning beet red. I guessed it was pretty embarrassing for a guy to have his mom hug him in front of everybody. But I figured, underneath, it was probably exactly what Ricardo needed.

"We're proud of your talents, son," Uncle Hector agreed and patted Ricardo on the back.

Aunt Inez finally let him out of her arms, and he scooted quickly away from her on the couch, looking like he wanted to shrivel up and fall through the space between the cushions. I exchanged a look with Xochitl. *Boys*. One minute they act all angry, the next they act all embarrassed, when really on the inside they're sad and then happy, just like us.

"Now, why didn't you tell me about your adventures, Isabel?" my mother asked. I suddenly felt ashamed. She had shared the secret of the *papel picado* with me, and I had been keeping all of these secrets from her just because I didn't want to get in trouble.

"We didn't want to worry you, Esperanza," Uncle Hector jumped in. "There was so much going on with the *quince*—we didn't want to tire you out."

Dad opened his mouth to speak, but Mom held up a hand to silence him. "Please. I will speak for myself. Listen to me now, all of you. Everyone loves to tell me how strong I am, and then at the very same time, treat me like I am some delicate, breakable object—like your glass eagle!" She paused. "I am no glass eagle. I am just me. A person with MS. A daughter, a sister, a wife, and especially a mother. And when something is going on with my children, I want to know. It's a mother's job to know." She smiled at me. "Deal?"

"Deal!" Everyone shouted.

"We never meant to offend you, Esperanza," Uncle Hector apologized. "It's only because we care about you."

"I know. And I thank you for your care. But I like caring for others too." I snuggled in next to my mom and looked around the room at my family and my new friends, Mr. Guerrero and Xochitl. Now that everybody knew everything, I felt like a huge weight was lifted off my shoulders . . . the weight of a giant glass eagle!

"Come," said Mr. Guerrero, standing up and stretching his long legs. "This has been a day of many secrets.

But I think the best secret of all will be what's hiding in the cave by your *tinaja*."

"We'll show you!" I said, springing up and grabbing Ricardo by the arm. "Let's go!"

```
To: 4kicks, flikchic, Kgirl, Skywriter
Subject: HOWDY!


Hola, amigas! I've been deep in the
heart of Texas with no access to the
REAL (?) world for days, and it's been
WILD! I've been trying to get in touch
with you guys 4-ever (really!), but
it'll take a SUPER SLEEPOVER to fill
you in on everything.

The quince was incredible, awesome,
and amazing. The ranch setting made
it feel like a movie! Maeve—you would
have demanded a cowgirl outfit. My
cousins showed us a great time and
everything went better than planned.
So much to say, more on that later.
IT WAS A BLAST!! Ave, your bro saved
the day. You have to ask him about
the cake he made!

Something really crazy happened to
me, long story, but here goes: My
```

cousin Ricardo and I went horseback
riding after dark (sounds nuts/it
was) and we got stranded in a storm.
Hid out in a cave and almost died of
thirst (not really). We killed time by
exploring and found an amazing thing:
PICTOGRAPHS BY AN ANCIENT CULTURE.
Yes, yours truly stumbled on a
perfectly preserved site with rock art
and artifacts. I made sketches, took
a photo. A friend's father (famous
artist!) brought over some scientists
and they're talking MAJOR DISCOVERY.
I am so excited to finally be telling
you this that I can hardly type! Can't
you see the headlines now? "Girl from
Boston Makes Major Art Discovery (with
the Help of Her Cousin)."

Yesterday Mr. G (artist), his daughter
(cool kid with a cool name—Xochitl),
my uncle, my coz, and a couple of
art historians checked out the place
again, and they confirmed it. Nobody's
ever seen anything like this so close
to San Antonio—it could cause a debate
about the current thinking on these
people (Lower Pecos River People).
OMG, I was scared out of my skin for

a while in the cave. And Quince-zilla
almost annihilated me! (That's another
story.)

And then there was the crazy thing
that happened to me that was NOT so
fun. Okay, you're not going to believe
this, but my cousins have this really
incredible art collection (including
a Diego Rivera—husband of Frida!)
and . . . I sorta kinda broke one of
the pieces! It was this beauuuuutiful
glass eagle. And OF COURSE the artist
was the same guy I already mentioned!
Double trouble. Ricardo was there when
it happened and we tried not telling
anybody for a while, but eventually
the secret got out. Last time I ever
try keeping something like that a
secret. BSG lesson: when u mess up, u
gotta 'fess up. Right away.

BSG—when we're ready for ranching and
roping and riding and eating the best
Mexican food, my aunt says Y'ALL COME
ON DOWN. Someday maybe we will. In the
meantime, hang on to your spurs cuz
when I get home I will have one heck
of a horse tale to tell! Hasta mañana,

muchachas! Lots o' luv, Lafrida.

And Avery, I think Elena Maria and
Scott . . . well, they might be in
love. They are holding hands right now
by the pool.

To be continued . . .

Isabel's Texas Two-Step

BOOK EXTRAS

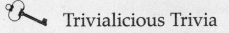 Trivialicious Trivia

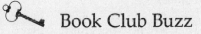 Book Club Buzz

 Texas Trivia

A Dilly of a 'Dillo

Isabel's Spanish-English Dictionary

Isabel's Texas Two-Step trivialicious trivia

1. What happens to Aunt Inez's eagle statue?
    A. It comes to life.
    B. Mercedes steals it.
    C. Isabel and Ricardo break the tip of its wing.
    D. Nothing

2. What is the name of the art gallery where Isabel meets Xochitl?
    A. The Mauve Squirrel
    B. The Blue Turtle
    C. The Green Flamingo
    D. The Red Cat

3. What does the rooster's name mean in English?
    A. Friendly
    B. Funky
    C. Fluffy
    D. Freckles

4. What has Mrs. Martinez been making for Elena Maria's *quinceañera*?
    A. Cookies
    B. Party hats
    C. Origami animals
    D. Photo frames

5. What kind of instrument does Ricardo play?
    A. Drums
    B. Accordion
    C. Clarinet
    D. Maracas

6. What is the name of Ricardo's horse?
    A. Silver
    B. Rasquatch
    C. Trigger
    D. Hidalgo

7. What do Ricardo and Isabel find in the cave?
   A. A family of armadillos
   B. A secret tunnel
   C. Buried treasure
   D. Painted pictographs

8. How did Isabel's parents meet?
   A. At a dance
   B. In a class at school
   C. In a coffee shop
   D. At a science-fiction convention

9. How does Scott save Elena Maria's *quinceañera*?
   A. He sings for her when the band quits.
   B. He bakes the cake after the cooks quit.
   C. He fixes her dress after it rips.
   D. He builds a platform for her to stand on.

10. What does Elena Maria give to Isabel?
    A. Her last doll
    B. A Frida Kahlo painting
    C. Her old shoes
    D. Flowers

Book Club Buzz

**10 QUESTIONS FOR YOU AND YOUR FRIENDS
TO CHAT ABOUT**

1. The *quinceañera* is a birthday tradition in
   Mexican culture. Does your culture have
   any birthday traditions? Does your family
   have any special birthday traditions?

2. Isabel and Ricardo admit to breaking the
   eagle statue because they are afraid that
   Mercedes will get in trouble for it. Have
   you ever been in a situation where you
   could have let someone else take the blame
   for your actions? What did you do? If
   you've never been in a situation like
   that, what would you do if you were?

3. Isabel gets upset when Elena Maria and her
   friends ignore her or make fun of her. If
   you have siblings, what do you do when

they are with their friends and you are feeling excluded?

4. No one in Isabel's family knew that her mother could make origami and *papel picado* until she revealed it at Elena Maria's *quinceañera*. Do you have any hidden talents?

5. Ricardo and Isabel get into big trouble when they leave the party without telling anyone. If you were in Isabel's place, would you have left the party with Ricardo? Why or why not?

6. Even though Isabel's mother suffers from multiple sclerosis, it's important to her to take an active role in planning for her daughter's big party. Do you know anyone with a serious illness? How do they cope with it? If it affects you, how do you cope with it?

7. Ricardo plays the accordion because of its role in conjunto music, which is an important part of his Mexican heritage. Do you play any instruments? How are they significant to you or your heritage?

8. Isabel admires artists like Frida Kahlo and Cesar Guerrero. Who do you admire and why?

9. Aunt Inez took complete control over Elena Maria's *quinceañera*, even though she's only Elena Maria's aunt. What would you have done? Have you ever had to deal with a control freak? How did you deal?

10. When Ricardo and Isabel find the paintings in the cave, they don't tell anyone right away. Do you think this was the right thing to do? What would you have done?

Texas Trivia

An Ancient People

The Coahuiltecans were actually a large group made up of many different Native American tribes, all of whom inhabited Texas and parts of northern Mexico. The name "Coahuilteca" was based on the name of the area of Mexico, called Coahuila, that many of the tribes lived in.

On the Move

The Coahuiltecans were nomadic, meaning that they traveled from place to place in search of food. As hunter-gatherers, they hunted for animals and gathered wild plants to eat as they moved. Only men hunted for deer, but both men and women fished. To catch fish they would use nets, bows and arrows, or just their hands!

Mission: Alamo

The Alamo, originally called the Mission San Antonio de Valero, was built in 1722. Before it was used as a military fort, it functioned as a church. Today, the Alamo is a museum, and a group called the Daughters of the Republic of Texas is responsible for its maintenance and upkeep.

A Royal History

The city of San Antonio started out as a small settlement called the Royal Presidio of San Antonio de Béjar (try saying that three times fast!). It was established in 1718, and was originally designed to defend the Mission San Antonio de Valero—aka, the Alamo.

Saintly Origins

San Antonio is named after Saint Anthony of Padua. On June 13, 1619, Spanish explorers celebrated Saint Anthony's feast day in the area. They named it San Antonio, which is Spanish for Saint Anthony, in honor of the saint.

Art Alert

The church at Mission Concepción is the only mission church in San Antonio that has never been seriously damaged as a result of bad weather. Because of this, it still contains some of the original frescos that were painted inside of it when it was first built more than 250 years ago!

My Kind of Party!

San Antonians hold a superhuge celebration called Fiesta San Antonio every year in April. The Fiesta lasts for ten whole days and is full of parades, carnivals, feasts, and art exhibits!

Texan-in-Chief

Four U.S. presidents were Texans: Dwight D. Eisenhower, Lyndon B. Johnson, George H. W. Bush, and George W. Bush.

Lone but Not Lonely

Texas's nickname, "The Lone Star State," comes from the design of the state flag, which shows a single five-pointed star.

Saddle Up!

America's first-ever rodeo was held in Pecos, Texas, on July 4, 1883, when a couple of cowboys decided to find out who could rope calves and ride bulls and broncos the best. When more cowboys found out about the competition, they joined right in. Pretty soon, people were lining up to watch! Every summer, the town of Pecos still holds an annual rodeo. Yee-haw!

A Dilly of a 'Dillo

An Avery Madden Crazy Critters Exclusive

Hey there, animal fans! Avery here, chatting with Sassafras, the nine-banded armadillo—the only species of armadillo that lives in the United States! Sassafras and most of her relatives are from Texas, but she's also got cousins in Oklahoma, Louisiana, Arkansas, Mississippi, and Florida.

Avery Madden: So, Sassafras, there's something I've just been dying to know. Are armadillos reptiles? I mean, you've got scales all over you, so . . .

Sassafras Armadillo: To tell you the truth, Avery, I'm a mammal. Those scales make up my shell, which has nine bands. It protects me, and it's actually how I got my name. *Armadillo* is Spanish for "armored one."

AM: Wow, really?

SA: *¡Sí, sí!* When I curl up, nothing can get me! Armadillos are the only mammal that has an exoskeleton.

AM: An exo-what?

SA: An exoskeleton. You have your skeleton inside of your skin, but I have one on the inside and on the outside. My shell is made out of bone.

AM: You know, I think my science teacher mentioned exoskeletons once. Insects have them, right?

SA: *Sí.* Speaking of insects, I'm getting kind of hungry.

AM: You eat bugs? Cool!

SA: If there are a lot around. We armadillos are pretty chill—if we can't find what we want, we'll settle for second best. My favorite foods are insects, spiders, and small amphibians, but I'll eat berries and plants too.

AM: Now, I know this is a sensitive subject, but . . . is there

anything out there that would like
to eat *you*?

> SA: Gotta love that law of the jungle.
> I have to be on the lookout for pumas,
> birds of prey, and snakes.

AM: Yikes! Well, you don't have
to worry about my snake, Walter.
He's completely harmless. Anyway, Sassafras, do you have any
siblings?

> SA: You better believe it! I'm actually a
> quadruplet. I have three sisters named
> Tammy, Pammy, and Cammy.

AM: Wow! Quadruplets! Has
People magazine called for a cover
shot?

> SA: Nah, it's nothing special. Most
> armadillos give birth to identical qua-
> druplets.

AM: You mean you and your
sisters look exactly the same?

SA: *Sí.* My sisters and I are so alike, Mom and Dad can't tell us apart most of the time. It drives them crazy!

AM: So I guess you don't get your own room.

SA: Nope. I have to share with Tammy, Pammy, and Cammy. Luckily I don't have to share with my older brothers: Lester, Sylvester, Chester, and Jimbo!

Isabel's Spanish-English Dictionary

abrazo: hug

abuelito/abuelita: grandfather/grandmother

acequia: irrigation ditch

aeropuerto: airport

Americanas: Americans

amigo/amiga: friend

Ándale: Get a move on

animalitos: little animals

¡Ay!: Oh!

azúcar: sugar

bailador: dancer

balcón: balcony

bolsa: bag

Buenas noches: Good night

Buenas tardes: Good afternoon

Buenos días: Good day

chambelanes: at a *quinceañera*, the boys who escort the damas on the honor court; literally, "Chamberlains"

chambelan de honor: honor escort

chica: girl

chiles rellenos: spicy stuffed chiles

chinampa: land created in a body of water by piling up mud; part of a landfill system used by the Aztecs

chiquita: little girl

chula: cutie or darling

Claro que sí: Certainly

cocinero: cook

cocina: kitchen

conjunto: genre of music developed in the Mexican-American communities of Texas; literally, "ensemble"

corte de honor: the group of boys and girls who stand by the *quinceañera* at her celebration; literally, "court of honor" or "honor court"

Cuida a tu mamá: Take care of your mother

damas: the girls who stand by the *quinceañera* at her celebration; literally, "ladies"

¡Dios mío!: My God!

Don: Mr.

Doña: Mrs.

¿Dónde está . . . ?: Where is . . . ?

empanadas: small pies, like turnovers

entrada: entrance

¿Esa música, que es?: That music, what is it?

fiesta: party

flautas: long tortillas filled with chicken or beef, rolled up, and fried; literally, "flutes"

fuera: out, outside

fuerza: force; strength

gallo: rooster

Gracias: Thank you

gran entrada: grand entrance

grito: shout, scream, yell

harina: flour

Hasta mañana: See you tomorrow

hermana: sister

hermanita: little sister

hijo/hija: son/daughter

huevos: eggs

La Llorona: a Mexican folktale that features a sad "weeping woman"

Le llama . . .: Its name is . . .

loco/loca: mad, crazy

magnífico: magnificent

mamacita: dear girl; literally, "little mother"

mantequilla: butter

Me gusto mucho el chocolate: I like chocolate very much

mi amor: My love

mi amorcita: my little love

mi hijita, mi 'jita: my little daughter

mi hijo/mi 'jo: my son

mi muñequita: my little doll

Mira esta muchachita: Look at this little girl

muchacha: girl

muchachita: little girl

muchacho: boy

Muchas gracias: Thank you very much

mujeres: women

música: music

Muy buen hecho: Very well done

muy bueno: very good

Muy travieso, ese gallo, el Pecas: Very mischievous, that rooster, Freckles

niña: girl

padrino/madrino: godfather/godmother; at a *quinceañera*, family members or family friends who sponsor certain aspects of the celebration

papel picado: Mexican paper art that involves cutting out patterns; literally, "minced paper"

pecas: freckles

preciosa: precious

presidio: fort

primo/prima: cousin

Que bonito: How pretty, How nice

Que demonios!: What demons!

Que hermosa!: What beauty!

queso: cheese

rancheras: folk songs from Mexico

ranchito: small ranch

rancho: ranch

sala: living room

Salud!: Cheers!

Señor: Mr.

sí: yes

taller: workshop

tamales: filled corn tortillas, steamed inside a corn husk

tlacuache: possum

tinaja: natural swimming hole made of rock; literally, "large earthen jar"

tío/tía: uncle/aunt

Toma: Take this; drink this

travieso: mischievous; making trouble

Venga: Come

verdad: truth

viejita: little old woman

Here's an excerpt from the

BEACON STREET GIRLS

next adventure,
Green Algae and Bubblegum Wars

It was a gorgeous, sunny day, but Maeve Kaplan-Taylor was not a happy camper. There was nothing quite as upsetting as watching her four best friends happily turn down Beacon Street on their way to their favorite hangout, Montoya's Bakery, without her. Katani, in her shiny silver-colored parka, was strutting ahead confidently. She was telling Charlotte and Isabel all about a fabulous sale going on at her favorite vintage store. Avery was jogging along behind the other three, happily dribbling a blue and yellow soccer ball. But Maeve, sadly, was left standing alone. *Now I know how that cheese must have felt in the song about the Farmer in the Dell. Poor little cheese!* Maeve thought to herself, dramatically touching her heart.

"Hey, Maeve, last chance—we really want you to come!" Avery hollered back, stopping her soccer ball under her sneaker. She beckoned for Maeve to join the group. "Think about it—a mug full of Montoya's chocolate deliciousness . . . ?"

"Oh, I really, really *do* want to go! But I just can't—it's my tutoring day. Have a mug for me, okay?"

"Okay!" Avery shouted. And with that she punted her soccer ball up the street and took off in a wild chase behind it.

Maeve felt like there were lead blocks attached to her feet as she trudged back to her family's apartment on Harvard Street. After all, this had been a bad, horrible day right from the start. It all began when Maeve overslept for the second time that week and had to run to school without breakfast or major hair repair. A triple tragedy.

Then worst of all, Ms. Rodriguez had given the class a pop quiz in English. Maeve hated pop quizzes more than anything . . . even more than practicing free throws in basketball. Studying for a regular test was bad enough, but to be *ambushed* with a test . . . right when she was *starving* . . . that was just too unfair! And . . . lunch, of course, was none other than the dreaded tuna fish mac and cheese—maybe the worst thing ever invented. A cup of hot chocolate and some quality time with the BSG probably would have been the one thing that could've cheered her up.

The tiny silver lining on Maeve's ginormous black rain cloud was her ultra-cute math tutor, Matt. *Matt, Matt, Matt.* Maeve thought he looked like Caleb Tucker, the adorable actor from *Maplewood,* one of her absolute fave TV shows. Plus Matt was a student at Boston College. Compared to the immature boys in her class like Henry Yurt and Billy Trentini, Matt the Adorable was a dream. In Maeve's personal opinion, all tutors should have to be adorable by law. *Oh!*

Lightbulb moment, Maeve thought excitedly. Maybe Matt the Adorable could even make her *want* to learn science like Charlotte and Katani—they were both crazy about math and science.

When she arrived home, she was relieved to see that Matt hadn't arrived yet. *Phew.* Now she had a chance to have a snack and freshen up a little. As soon as she opened the kitchen door, a heavenly smell wafted her way. *Cookies— chocolate chip cookies.* From the plastic wrapper on the counter she saw that it was the kind from a big block of pre-made dough. Maeve's mother worked and didn't have too much time to make cookies from scratch, but Maeve didn't care one bit. Cookie dough was cookie dough. Period, final. Next to the plastic wrapper she saw a note in her mother's handwriting: "Hi, Maeve—I'm on a conference call in my bedroom— cookies will be done at 3:15—work hard with Matt! XOXO Love, Mom."

"Hey, Maeve! Think fast!"

Maeve didn't have time to think at all, because something hard—very hard—suddenly smacked her in the chest. "Ouch!" she cried, watching a plastic ball roll away. *That really hurt,* she thought angrily. Maeve knew just who was responsible: with fiery blue eyes, she charged toward the sound of muffled laughter behind the china cabinet. Sure enough, there was her little brother, Sam, curled up on the floor, obviously pretending to be some kind of ninja Army dude—his favorite pastime other than torturing his older sister.

"What is *your* problem?" Maeve said, sounding every bit as annoyed as she felt.

"Huh? What'd I do?" Sam blinked innocently.

"Don't play dumb with me, Sam. You threw that ball at me for no reason. *Hard!* And guess what? It really hurt!"

Sam's smile disappeared when he saw that his sister wasn't joking around. Sam liked to tease Maeve—okay, Sam *loved* to tease Maeve—but he never meant to hurt her. "I'm sorry," Sam mumbled. "I was just joking around. I thought you would laugh."

Maeve shook her head. How her brother ever thought that whacking her with a hard plastic ball would be funny was completely beyond her. "Oh, yeah? You know what makes people laugh?" Maeve asked.

Sam shrugged. "Um . . . what?"

Maeve mischievously raised an eyebrow. "You really wanna know?"

Sam nodded.

"Usually, this works every time." Maeve wiggled her fingers and went in for the kill, tickling her brother until Sam shrieked with laughter.

"I need rescue!" Sam yelled.

Suddenly, a male voice spoke from behind the pair of giggling kids. "Is this a bad time, Maeve?"

Startled, Maeve looked up and brushed her red ringlets out of her face. *Oops!* Just her luck! Matt the Adorable had arrived. Usually, Maeve strived to act like the glamorous future movie star that she knew in her heart she was. Why did Matt have to catch her playing with her little brother?

Sam jumped up like a Mexican jumping bean, while Maeve slowly peeled herself off the linoleum kitchen floor.

"Hey, Matt, wanna see my new Astro fighter plane?" Sam asked.

"Psst. Out of here, Sam! Matt's here to help me, okay?" Maeve whispered fiercely. She glided over to the oven, used the heavy mitts to slide out the tray, and flashed her best camera-ready smile. "Would you care for a pastry, Matt?" she asked, as she transferred the cookies to a rack. "Pastry" sounded way more sophisticated than "cookie."

"Yeah, cool! Thanks, Maeve." He eagerly took two and gobbled them down. Maeve looked at him and thought dreamily, *This is just what it would be like if we were married. He'd get home from work. I would have a warm snack all ready and waiting. And I'd be wearing a little dress with short puffy sleeves and a red and white checkered apron, and my hair would be pulled back in a ponytail with a big red bow . . .* Maeve's daydreams were snapshots captured from all the old movies she watched on Saturdays at the movie theater her dad ran, which, lucky for her, was right below her apartment.

"Hey, Earth to Maeve, are you ready to get cracking on your science homework?" Matt asked, shattering her delightful fantasy.

"Science, shmience," Maeve groaned. "How about, let's not and say we did?"

"How about, your Mom would fire me?"

Maeve's eyes widened and she shook her head, feeling her curls brush her face. "Oh, no! I would never let *that* happen." She sighed, reluctantly slung her pink backpack onto the kitchen table, and pulled out her pink science binder. Maeve reasoned that if you had to do school stuff, you might as well surround yourself in pink. She once saw an interior design show that explained how the color pink put people in an optimistic frame of mind.

"I have bad news, Matt. I mean—really, really, extraordinarily, super-duperously . . . um . . ."

Matt raised his eyebrows. "Bad?"

"Yeah." She pulled out a sheet of paper and held it against her chest for a moment. She was sure that showing it to Matt would result in the end of the world.

"Okay, let's see it, Maeve. Is it another C?"

Maeve blushed, a little embarrassed that *that* was Matt's first thought. "No . . . *worse*," she moaned as she slapped the paper down on the table.

On the top, in bold letters, the page read ABIGAIL ADAMS JUNIOR HIGH SCIENCE FAIR.

"This is, like, the ultimate tragedy."

Matt muffled a burst of laughter. "Is that a fact? If I remember correctly, didn't you tell me just last week that *Romeo and Juliet* was the ultimate tragedy?"

"I mean in my own life, Matthew." Maeve rolled her eyes, but secretly loved how Matt was joking with her . . . maybe even . . . *flirting*? She wasn't positive, but she made a mental note to ask the BSG later. "We both know that science stuff is hard enough for me as it is. But did you read this thing? It says I need to do an *experiment*. *An experiment!* Who do they think I am? Albert Armstrong?"

"You mean, Albert Einstein?"

Maeve flipped her hair. "*Whatever*. Science and drama girls like me do not mix. Well, most of the time, anyway," she added, not wanting to sound like a complete doof in front of this dreamy college boy. "I mean, really, what am I supposed to do an experiment on—if my hair looks better curly or straight? Please."

Matt leaned his head forward and sighed. Maeve wondered if she had gone too far, even for her. But Matt popped back up again and said, "Okay, Maeve, chill time. This is totally doable. First of all, girls can be great at science, and if you don't believe me, then you've got to go to the Sally Ride Science Festival for girls. It's at MIT this weekend and it is going to be seriously interesting."

Before Maeve even had a chance to say, *More science? I don't think so, . . .* Matt had taken a brochure out of his bag. "Check it out."

Maeve expected to see snapshots of a drab gymnasium full of boring-looking posters and homemade volcanoes. But the pictures of the fair were outdoors, right by the Charles River overlooking Boston. There were girls everywhere and huge booths filled with colors. *This doesn't look like a boring science festival to me.* Maeve looked at Matt suspiciously. There was even a close-up that showed a group of girls trying on lip gloss.

Collect all the BSG books today!

#10 Just Kidding

The BSG are looking forward to Spirit Week at Abigail Adams Junior High, until some mean—and untrue—gossip about Isabel dampens everyone's spirits.

#11 Ghost Town

The BSG's fun-filled week at a Montana dude ranch includes skiing, snowboarding, cowboys, and celebrity twins—plus a ghost town full of secrets.

#12 Time's Up

Katani knows she can win the business contest. But with school and friends and family taking up all her time, has she gotten in over her head?

#13 Green Algae and Bubble Gum Wars

Inspired by the Sally Ride Science Fair, the BSG go green, but getting stuck slimed by some gooey supergum proves to be a major annoyance!

Also ... Our Special Adventure Series:

Charlotte in Paris

Something mysterious happens when Charlotte returns to Paris to search for her long-lost cat and to visit her best Parisian friend, Sophie.

Maeve on the Red Carpet

A cool film camp at the Movie House is a chance for Maeve to become a star, but newfound fame has a downside for the perky redhead.

Freestyle with Avery

Avery Madden can't wait to go to Telluride, Colorado, to visit her dad! But there's one surprise that Avery's definitely not expecting.

Katani's Jamaican Holiday

A lost necklace and a plot to sabotage her family's business threaten to turn Katani's dream beach vacation in Jamaica into stormy weather.

Isabel's Texas Two-Step

A disastrous accident with a valuable work of art and a sister with a diva attitude give Isabel a bad case of the ups and downs on a special family trip.

Tell your BFFs to meet you on Beacon Street!

Join the Tower Club at **BeaconStreetGirls.com** for Super-cool virtual sleepovers and parties! Personalize your locker and get $5.00 to spend on Club BSG gifts with this secret code

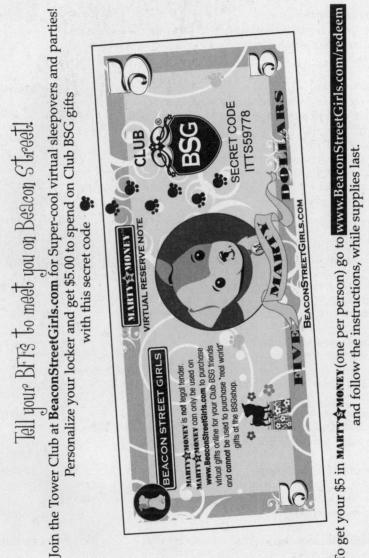

To get your $5 in **MARTY'S MONEY** (one per person) go to **www.BeaconStreetGirls.com/redeem** and follow the instructions, while supplies last.